The Five Points

The Five Points

Rocco Dormarunno

Writers Club Press
San Jose New York Lincoln Shanghai

The Five Points

Writers Club Press
an imprint of iUniverse, Inc.

For information address:
iUniverse, Inc.
5220 S. 16th St., Suite 200
Lincoln, NE 68512
www.iuniverse.com

ISBN: 0-595-20446-5

Printed in the United States of America

This book is dedicated to my wife, Jenny, whose love and support gave me the confidence to finally get this work done! God knows she's been patient with me.

Preface

"Let us go again and plunge into the Five Points. This is place...all that is loathsome, drooping and decayed is here."

Charles Dickens
American Notes for General Circulation, 1842

BOOK ONE

THE TRAMP
(1860)

He jumped down from the train as it slowed into its final turn. After regaining his composure, he gripped tightly the handle of his suitcase and hobbled east along 47th Street. It was just after midnight, he judged, because he had hopped onto the train almost an hour earlier in Dobbs Ferry. The grandfather clock in the house that he'd been in told him it was 10:55 when he left. The house in Dobbs Ferry was only a two-minute walk to the tracks, and the black train with lime trim had been huffing right there, as if waiting for him.

As he continued along 47th Street, he could hear cows lowing from small black barns. It was the sound he'd heard all along his five-year trek from Ontario.

His name was Martine DelaCroix, a forty-two year old Canadian roamer. He was wanted by the law on two charges of burglary in Toronto in 1855. He was wanted on one charge of burglary and one charge of aggravated assault in Buffalo in 1856. There was a warrant for his arrest in connection with a robbery and homicide in Oneonta in 1858. In 1859, he was wanted on

1

three charges of assault and battery and two charges of armed robbery in Wappingers Falls, and was wanted for questioning in connection with the murder of a schoolteacher in Suffern. It was April 18, 1860. By the next morning, he would be wanted for the murders of a young widow and her two sons who had lived and died in the house in Dobbs Ferry.

Martine had always made a decent livelihood through his burglaries and robberies, and had considered violence counterproductive: it shortened his escape time and would lengthen a jail sentence. But in the last few years, the bloodshed mounted. Sometimes he garroted or stabbed or broke the necks of his victims without even taking their money. He didn't know why the demons compelled him to do these things. At times, Martine was remorseful, but those moments of remorse were often catalysts for new violence.

Martine had never been to New York City, but knew he'd end up there some day. The word among the tramps that rode in boxcars or on top of freight trains was: there were no jobs in New York; the gangs were vicious; nobody cared about hoboes; and Manhattan was too crowded.

These were considered assets to Martine: he'd make his own jobs; he was tough enough to link up with any gang; being a hobo, nobody would pay him any mind; and, in crowds, Martine judged he'd never be found.

Martine was not a big man: five foot five, around 140 pounds, none of it fat. That was just about the only correct aspect the police descriptions had of him. He had shaved off his "curly black beard" and trimmed his "bushy" black eyebrows. He no longer dressed in a "disheveled fashion": he kept the clothes he stole, or bought with stolen money, clean. His wardrobe he kept in a new leather suitcase. Unlike other tramps that terrorized rural and suburban towns, Martine was hardly given a second look as he wandered down the dusty roads of upstate New York. Grim-faced and tight-lipped, Martine looked more like an inconvenienced salesman dragging his wares than a tramp and fugitive. The only telltale feature he could not hide was his terrible limp, caused by buckshot fragments embedded behind his right kneecap. Those fragments had been there since he was eleven, when his mother's demons had shot him for forgetting to feed the cows on their little farm.

When he reached the East River, he rested briefly. Unlike the Hudson, which seemed as purple and wide and deep and tranquil as any lake in the Canada of his youth, this narrow, black rush of water greased by with a frenzy that Martine could only liken to a burglar escaping a home which had discovered his presence. It was determined to run, to get to somewhere else—indifferent of where the path might lead. It just had to move and move.

Martine looked to the south. In the distance, he could see where clusters of gaslamps cast amber fogs over certain pockets of the city. He picked up his suitcase and walked towards them. When he later neared Canal Street, the stench of horse manure and rotting fish along the waterfront made Martine gag. He was amazed at the number of children who slept on bales of hay amid this reeking refuse.

At one-thirty in the morning, he arrived in The Five Points, which was where he wanted to be. Martine had heard all the stories about the place. The alcoholics slept in the gutters, prostitutes advertised their services, thugs everywhere, gambling everywhere: he'd seen it all before, just not as concentrated. He was not impressed and he was not afraid. As he walked by Paradise Square and the crumbling brick, wood, and clapboard structures around it, Martine could hear the blare of off-key music and the shouts of drunken passions. Foul and stagnant fumes, worse than that of the decomposing fish at Canal Street, almost compelled the tramp to raise his handkerchief to his nose, but he dared not.

Its reputation was near mythical: there was no place darker, no place lower, no place poorer, no place so infested with danger and pain than The Five Points, Martine had heard. This was the confluence of all human dishonesty, the epicenter of all depravity, the rock-hard cradle of earthly misery. No area of hell itself was believed to provoke more fear among the so-called reputable people, nor spawn more admiration among the so-called dangerous classes than The Five Points. And with each agonizing step, Martine began to realize why.

"Here, hell-bitch!" Martine heard a woman scream from the second-storey window of a tenement. "Get away from my door!"

Martine looked and saw a prostitute loitering by the building's entranceway. Her exposed breasts were smeared with muddy fingerprints. She looked up at the first woman and shouted back, "Haven't you had enough, you old whore? Save some for the rest of us!"

"I've got something saved fer ye!" the woman in the window fired back. She disappeared from view momentarily. When she returned, she brandished an ice pick. "I got this for you! And I'm coming down to stick ye with it!"

Martine hurried along, deciding it would be best not to witness anything more. As he turned a corner, he was nearly bowled over by a wild pig and the two little boys chasing after it with broken bottles. Cross Street was particularly treacherous for Martine, as it was coated with slime, mud, and manure. Most of the gas lamps on this street were either smashed or in such a state of neglect that they provided little illumination for the tramp. In the thickest darkness, a sudden fear iced his feet, as it did whenever the demons appeared. Figures flickered in the corners of his eyes and then vanished.

But they were not demons, Martine realized. The unconnected two- and three-storied houses and shacks barely concealed the wobbly, dilapidated shanties behind them. In some places, the shanties had been hastily constructed between buildings. Martine saw a nude woman, either drunk or beaten, crawl on all-fours from out of a shanty and disappear behind a warehouse. On the other side of the street, Martine saw a one-legged man stare back at him.

Two more black pigs ran squealing toward the tramp but nobody was pursuing them this time. He put down his suitcase and hitched up his trousers. He was tired. Although his determination to continue his surveillance told him to keep walking, his weak knee argued persuasively against it. He turned another corner, hoping to find a rooming house.

A large, young man in his late teens staggered to him. He was drunk: not a happy, oblivious drunk, but a mean one. He stepped in Martine's way. "Hey crip, what's in the bag?"

Martine answered plainly, "Clothes." He could see that the whites of the boy's eyes were blood red.

"Fancy clothes, eh?" the young man asked. "You look like a fancy man."

"Just clothes," Martine said.

"Just clothes," the teen echoed. He belched. "Have you got any money in that bag? You look like a fancy man who carries all his money in a big bag. Are you a Mister Money Bags?"

Martine gave a quick glance over his shoulder, making sure the drunken boy wasn't a diversion for a garrotter from behind. "No, I am not. Please, I must be going, now. Excuse me." He tried to pass the boy, but his path was blocked.

"Now, where are you off to, Mr. Money Bags? We just met." He pulled out a knife. "I need a loan, Mr. Money Bags. Let me have your money."

Martine eyed the knife briefly. Then he looked the boy in his eyes. "Put that away, child. You can hurt yourself."

The boy laughed. "Hoo! Mr. Money Bags is a tough bloke, isn't he?"

Martine noticed that two prostitutes were watching the exchange from across the street. A middle-aged man observed everything from the second floor window of a crumbling brick home.

"No, child," Martine explained, "I'm not a tough man. I'm just a smart one."

The boy's face reddened. "Stop calling me a child, you bastard!"

"Very well, then," Martine said. "Put that knife away, young man."

The boy nodded, "O, I'll put this knife away. I'll put it away in your bloody heart!"

Martine blocked the knife thrust with his suitcase. As the boy wrestled to pull the knife out, Martine spat in his eyes. He dropped his suitcase, grabbed the boy by the hair and slammed his face into his good knee.

"Good kick!" the middle-aged man hollered from his window.

The boy, stunned, dropped to the ground. Martine jumped upon the boy's kidneys. And then, swiftly, he placed him in a headlock. A serpentine creature materialized on Martine's arm. It bore the battered head of an old woman. It hissed, "I want his blood!"

The middle-aged man leaned further out the window. "Go on, break the bastard's neck!"

Martine, however, did not require such coaching. With a jerking twist, the deed was done. The boy's body went limp. Martine stood up and brushed himself off.

"Nicely done," the middle-aged man said. He applauded. "That little bastard was a menace even to this neighborhood. You've done us a service. Thank you."

Martine looked up and nodded. "You're welcome," he said.

The prostitutes rushed across the street and swooped down on the boy. One removed the boy's leather belt and shoes, the other confiscated his pockets for the few pennies he had in them. She stood up with twelve copper coins in her hands and looked at Martine.

Although she didn't offer it, Martine shook his head in reply. "I don't want his money. You keep it."

"Say, friend," the man called down from his window. "You're new in the area, aren't you?"

"Yes," Martine said.

"Do you need a job?"

Martine shrugged. "Just like everyone else, I suppose."

The middle-aged man lit a pipe. "See the haberdasher's shop on the corner there? Off the corner of Baxter? That's mine. Come by tomorrow, and I'll give you work. The name's Ike Croft."

"Thank you," Martine said. "Thank you, Mr. Croft."

"You're welcome," Ike said. Then he asked, "Have you a place to stay the night?"

Martine shook his head. "I thought I'd find a boarding house."

"There's a flophouse just up a block," Ike replied. "Mrs. Mooney is the owner. She's up all hours of the night, so don't worry about calling upon her so late. Anyway, her shotgun keeps people honest."

Martine smiled. "Thank you, again." Martine watched the prostitutes cease their looting of the fallen boy. They ambled back to their positions beside the gas lamp across the road. Martine decided he was going to like the area. Then a thought suddenly occurred to him. Martine said to Ike, "But, sir, I don't know anything about haberdashery."

Ike removed the pipe from his mouth and smiled. As he reached up to close the window, he replied, "Good! Neither do I!"

*   *   *

"Ye got me money, Captain?" Petey Daley, the diminutive leader of The Dead Rabbits asked. He and ten of his men stood in an alleyway off Henry Street.

The elderly, well-dressed man in the dark brown carriage was protected by two men armed with rifles; the driver had two .38s holstered to his hips. "Here," the well-dressed man said, tossing an envelope to Petey Daley. "Five hundred. Remember, Tammany doesn't care how many B'hoys get beaten—just make sure The Butcher is finished."

"The bloody Orangeman won't get out alive," Petey answered with a smile, as he flipped through the bills. Petey Daley, called "Wee Petey", though never to his face, was barely over five feet tall with boyish looks. In fact, even after his 20th birthday, he could pass himself off as a pre-adolescent. After each countless arrest for street fighting, he had been sent to children's work-houses instead of adult penitentiaries. It was in those workhouses where he recruited many a young soldier. "Should be fun busting up another Bowery Boy joint."

"Tammany doesn't care about fun, Mr. Daley," the man admonished. "Elections are in two weeks. Just take care of Butcher Toole." Then he barked to the driver, "Get me the hell out of here."

Still smiling, Petey watched the handsome carriage bounce along the broken alleyway, as it raced away. He cried after it,

"God's speed, Captain!" Then little Petey turned to his crew, "Well, men, tis time to go to work."

Some of the grimy mob slipped on their brass knuckles. A few of them removed the sledgehammers they had concealed under their tattered greatcoats. Their tall cloth hats were stuffed with newspaper and rags to absorb any blows to the head they might suffer.

Hired thug, the burly Black Roger, so dubbed because of the condition of his remaining teeth, stepped up to The Dead Rabbits' leader, "Say, was that really Captain Rynders?"

Petey shrugged. "I dunno. He says he is. Says he's the real leader of The Dead Rabbits—the one who pulls all the levers in Tammany. Meanwhile I never seen him around when I have to organize things here. Unless his face is on a coin or bill, anybody can say who he is and I wouldn't be any bloody wiser. So long as he pays me, I don't care a spit." He spat. Then he showed Black Roger the contents of the envelope. "But these faces are very familiar to me, friend. And I know *they* are real." He handed Black Roger thirty dollars.

After pocketing the money, Roger asked, "How many Boys ye figure are in the club, Petey?"

The little man shrugged again, "Dunno. Ten, twenty, mebbe. It doesn't matter: we got the drop on 'em, so they won't be expecting us. Tis all we need." He pulled a revolver from the waist of his pants. Satisfied that all the chambers were loaded, Petey announced, "Time's a-wasting, men. Let's go!"

*   *   *

Mrs. Mooney's flophouse was just that: dirty, no furniture, no windows, just rows upon rows of bunks for people to flop on and sleep. No extra charges for lockers or screens—just a nickel for a spot on the floor or on a bunk. In one corner of the room sat a chamber pot and porcelain ewer of water.

Martine considered washing up but realized he'd only get dirty again from sleeping on the dusty mat. He put his suitcase under his head as a pillow.

There weren't many other people in the house: a family of Jews slept by a far wall; an Italian man smoked a small cigar in a corner of the room; and two Irishmen played cards by a kerosene lamp in the center.

Mrs. Mooney explained to Martine that during warm weather, poor people tended to sleep on the rooftops of abandoned buildings, rather than pay the extra nickel for a flophouse. "But 'tis fortunate ye came now, instead of, say, January," she had said. "Ye never would've gotten a spot this late at night in winter."

Martine judged Mrs. Mooney to be a kindly woman, not at all the type to run such a place in New York's most dangerous neighborhood. Then again, he realized, not everyone here had to be dishonest, not everyone had to be criminal. Some people could rise above it. However, Martine did make note of the shotgun she kept behind her desk.

Martine had the feeling that had he not just killed a man, and a woman and her two young boys earlier, the demons in his soul might have compelled him to kill Mrs. Mooney. For her sake, he decided, he would not return to the flophouse after that night.

*   *   *

Richard "The Butcher" Toole stood at the bar in The Bowery Boys' dingy, dimly-lit club. One foot atop the seldomly-polished brass foot rail, the big man—6 feet four inches tall, 240 pounds—wiped the sweat off his cleanly-shaved head. He devoured three dozen oysters and started on his fifth beer. The Butcher then told two of his friends, Johnny the Spitter and Dago Bill, about what had happened to him that day. The trio was the only people at the bar; the others, about a half-dozen men, played cards at a table.

The Butcher said, "Four of them bloody papists, members of The Roach Guard I think they was, come up to the campaign headquarters fixing to scare the people. And I says to them, 'Say, what's the big idear you blokes coming to this neighborhood?' And they says, 'To hell with you, Toole. People here going to votes fer Tammany.' And I says, 'Is that a fact?' They says, 'Aye, now steps aside.'"

"They told *you* to step aside? Nerve!" Dago Bill laughed. He placed the mug of beer that he'd poured for The Butcher in front of his friend.

In three gulps, The Butcher polished off the beer. After he belched, he continued, "Nerve is right! So I walks up to one of them—the biggest one—and I slaps him off the side of his head. Open-handed, mind you: I didn't punch the papist bastard. And the bloke goes flying three feet in the air and lands on his rump. And then—now heed this—the bloke starts crying. Blubbering like a bloody woman. Har-har! 'Ye broke me head! Boo-hoo, boo-hoo! Ye broke me head!' he cries. Har! The three other blokes goes running to him to help him and carry him away. And I pulls out a post from the fence around the headquarters, and I goes up to them like I was going to chase them, and I hollers, 'Next time, you should say *please* when you wants me to step aside.' Har-har!"

"You showed them!" Dago Bill commented. He was about to pour another beer from the barrel when he heard a ruckus from the front door. He turned and saw Petey Daley and Black Roger standing at the entrance.

The Butcher turned and raised an eyebrow at the pair, "Well, well, you sees what happens when you leaves the front door open?

Any piece of shite just rolls on in. In this case, one little piece of shite, and one big piece of shite. What's on your mind, papist?"

The other Bowery Boys stopped playing cards and stood up. One pulled a crowbar from under the table.

Smiling, Petey cocked back his head and stuck his thumbs in his pockets. "Good to see ye, Butcher. Ye look fit, fer an ugly bastard. Tis a foul night and I was cold and thirsty. Is it all right if me and me friend warm ourselves and have a cocktail?"

Black Roger spat into the sawdust.

"And have your hide stinks up the joint? I thinks you should be on your way before I slugs you, Wee Petey," The Butcher warned.

The smile gradually vanished from Petey's face. "Don't ever call me that," he growled. Petey whipped the pistol out and fired one shot.

Although the heavy slug tore through The Butcher's left shoulder, the big man hardly flinched. He looked at the neat quarter-inch hole in the front of his jacket, and saw a small stream of blood trickle out. He felt the warmth of the exit wound on his back.

Johnny the Spitter dove for cover behind the bar. The Bowery Boy with the crowbar rushed Petey but was intercepted by the hulking Black Roger who pulled the rusted tool out of the Boy's grip. With a fierce backhand, he smashed out six of the Boy's teeth.

As the other Bowery Boys charged Petey, The Dead Rabbits who'd been waiting on the damp cobblestones raced into the club. Petey kept his revolver trained on The Butcher but could not get off a clear shot, as the line of fire was obstructed by flying tables, chairs, and men.

Finally lifting his foot from the brass rail, The Butcher looked over the melee and into the barrel of the smoking revolver in Petey's hand. "Bloody papist," he muttered. He walked toward the leader of The Dead Rabbits. "You little bastard."

"Keep coming, Orangeman, and see what you get," Petey dared. He fired, but the shot was deflected by a fist in the throng.

Dago Bill was picked up off the sawdust by Black Roger and thrown into the liquor shelves.

"Fight like a man!" The Butcher hollered, as he approached within ten feet of Petey Daley.

Johnny the Spitter was dragged out from behind the bar. A Dead Rabbit battered his shins and ankles with a sledgehammer. Mirrors were smashed, the bar was crushed, tables and chairs were reduced to splinters.

Petey fired again, hitting The Butcher in the gut. Toole dropped to one knee. "Papist shite!" he growled. He got back on his feet and staggered toward Petey. "Am I the only true American who can fight in here? Come on, boys!"

Kerosene was poured out of a lantern and onto the wood floor. A Dead Rabbit lit it.

Petey Daley stepped back two paces and fired, catching a piece of The Butcher's ear.

Butcher Toole kept coming. "Youse don't have enough bullets in that gun to stops me!"

However, Petey Daley proved him wrong: his fifth shot cracked into The Butcher's eyebrow and sprayed his brain out of the back of his head.

"Is that so?" Petey asked the corpse.

*   *   *

Ike Croft rose early, as was his habit. He rubbed the crust from his eyes and opened the window to let in some air. It was warm outside, and the sun rising over the green lands of Brooklyn would not be blocked by any clouds.

On the walkway below, the body of the young drunk still lay. Two starved mongrels ate away at the corpse's soft tissue. Ike grabbed an empty tobacco tin and hurled it at the dogs. "Get on!" he shouted. The dogs yipped as they fled. "I hope they cart the thing away today. I don't need the bastard rotting away under my window."

Ike filled his blue basin with water. He shaved carefully around his great, white mustache. Ike was 53 years old, but had gone grey when he was in his early 20s. However, he was very proud of his thick shock of grey hair, and kept it meticulously groomed and parted down the middle. His concern for appearances, on the other hand, did not extend to his waist, as he neared obesity. To him, though, his big belly was a sign of prosperity that announced to the world, "I'm fed, not like all you poor, starving sons of bitches."

When he was done shaving, he put on his cream-colored suit, placed his revolver in his waistband, grabbed his walking stick, and headed out. He breakfasted at Abie's, one of the few Jewish-owned businesses in the area. As he paid for his meal, Ike told Abie, "We might not like you Jews comin' to the neighborhood, but you make damned good pickled herring. Damned good!"

Abie put the coins into the till, and said, "Thank you, Mr. Croft. It's always a pleasure to serve you. Come again."

"You know I will," Ike replied. He reached over the counter and popped Abie soundly on the shoulder. "Good morning to you!"

Ike stepped out into the brilliant morning. "Ah! It will be a fine day!" he announced. "Morning to you, lad," he said to a young beggar. He gave the rag-tag boy a two-cent piece.

When he got to his shop, he found Martine there waiting for him. Martine looked as though he had slept well. "Here's my eager-beaver, well-rested and ready to work!" Ike said.

"Good morning, Mr. Croft," Martine said.

"Ike, call me Ike, for Christ's sake," he laughed. He fumbled through his key ring, and then unlocked the door. "I'd ask you for your name, but I know it'd be a lie. So, what should I call you?"

Martine stated, "My name is Martine, and that is not a lie. Why do you think I'd not tell the truth?"

After closing the door, Ike whispered, "Because what I saw you do last night was not the first time you did that. You're good at killing, aren't you? You don't have to answer. Anyway, we'll call you Martin. Use that name." Almost as an afterthought, Ike added in normal tones, "And since you're new to the area, I must give you a word to the wise. There are five points to The Five Points." Ike enumerated each item on his stubby fingers:

"Point One: Never steal a man's food, whiskey or woman—or else.

"Point Two: If you accept money to do a job, you do it—or else.

"Point Three: If you join a gang, stay loyal to that gang—or else.

"Point Four: If a copper wants information, you don't know any-thing—or else.

"Point Five: If you think you're big and powerful enough, you can try to forget Points One to Four. But I wouldn't recommend it. If you can remember that, you'll be just fine."

Martine nodded, grateful for the information. "Then perhaps you can also tell me what this stench is that seems to fill the air every place. It goes right from my nose and into my stomach."

Ike Croft shrugged. "Well, if you ask the old folks of the area, they'll tell you one of two things: either it's the Devil himself farting or it's the rotten water that parts of this neighborhood was built over. Personally, I think it's both. You see, this area was once all swampland. Then they filled in the muck and built fine houses. This place was once so fancy that George Washington himself lived here a while. But they didn't fill the muck in enough or didn't fill it in right. And about thirty, maybe forty years ago, everything began to sink, and smell. And as it sank, it got closer to hell and the Devil, making it easier for him to suck it down more and more. But the neighborhood is so vile, it upsets the poor bastard's tummy a wee bit and fills him with gas."

"Alo? Che cosa succede?" a shrill voice cried out. A small man, wearing a black vest over a white shirt, jumped up from behind a display cabinet. He held a short-barreled Winchester rifle.

"It's all right, Luigi. It's just me," Ike replied. "That's Luigi," he informed Martine. "Guards the place overnight."

"How are you, Signore Croft?" Luigi asked. Martine estimated that the guard was in his early 20s, struggling to grow a mustache, perhaps in emulation of his favorite employer.

"I'm fine," Ike said heartily. "I trust you had a good night."

"Si," Luigi replied. "Some boys try to break in but I show them gun, they go away."

"Very good, Luigi," Ike said. "This is Martin. He'll be working here."

"Ah, si!" Luigi said smiling. "How are you, Signore Martino?" He extended his small hand.

"Fine," Martine said, shaking Luigi's hand.

Ike went behind a counter of men's handkerchiefs and pulled out a cigar box.

"You pay me, now," Luigi requested.

"Yes, me pay you, now." Ike sighed. Then to Martine, he added, "Bloody I-ties always want their money right away." Then he laughed and gave Luigi five dollars.

"Grazie, Signore Croft," Luigi said. "You are, how you say, generous man."

"I know," Ike said. "Here," he said, giving Luigi an extra two bits, "get a nice cake to bring to your little lady."

"Ma signore! Mille grazie, un altra volta," Luigi said. He turned to Martine and said, "You like to work with Signore Croft.

He good man. You see! Arrivederci." Luigi put on his short-brimmed hat and strutted out of the shop.

Martine noted, "That's an awful good salary for the night watchman of a haberdasher's."

Ike grinned lasciviously, "Well, on some of those nights when he's watching my place, I'm watching his beautiful young wife—and then some—if you catch my drift." He winked.

Martine nodded. "I see." He surveyed the tiny shop. There wasn't much in it—nothing at all except a few glass display cases with men's accessories: hats, pocket watch chains, cravats, and brushes. Most of the goods were long out of style, some of them going back to the forties. Otherwise it was a dust-covered empty room, like a neglected exhibit in a museum. "So, Ike, what are my duties and what are my wages?" he asked. "You aren't hiring me for my haberdashery skills, after all."

"That's right," Ike said. "I'm not." He took a key from the key ring. "Come with me, son."

Martine followed Ike to the back of the shop, where there was a heavy, mahogany door labeled "Office." Martine discovered, after the door was opened, that it was not an office at all. It was a large storeroom, filled with stolen goods. Two large crates were stenciled "FURS". Two others were loaded with brass candlesticks. Other cartons, mostly unmarked, were stacked in neat piles along the floor. "You're a fence," Martine observed.

"That's right," Ike said proudly. "And a damned good one. You will soon meet my young partners, Kid Gas and Hungry Frank." He walked over to a smaller crate and pulled out a handgun. "Here. You'll need this if you're going to work for me."

Martine refused the weapon. "No. I don't use those. Do you have a knife?"

Ike inspected the gun, as if something were wrong with it. He shrugged and dropped it back into the crate. "A man who likes to work with his hands, eh? I like that. I should have known." He rummaged through another small carton and pulled out an ivory-handled, three-inch knife. "Too small?"

"No," Martine answered. "Just right." He stuffed the knife into his boot. "I would like to ask you something."

"Go on," Ike said.

Martine asked, "Why does a fence need a hired killer?"

"I don't," Ike replied. "But I just need to know that my men are prepared for the worst, and aren't afraid to kill." He smiled.

But Martine could read the message behind the smile: "The worst does come from time to time, and I will ask you to kill for me." Martine shook his head. "I'm sorry to disappoint you, Mr. Croft, but I'm not a hired killer, in spite of what you saw last night. However, I have a different specialty."

"And what might that be?" Ike asked.

"Burglary," Martine responded. "I'm good."

"Good!?" Ike laughed. "You had better be more than 'good' to work in this area," Ike informed Martine. "This neighborhood is loaded with the best: some of The Whyos, some of The Dead Rabbits—all of The Daybreak Boys—they're the best! I'm sorry, son, but good isn't good enough. I can't help you. But I still can use you to mind things around here during the day. Help me keep the inventory."

Again Martine shook his head. "I am not cut out to be a book-keeper." Then he offered, "Sir, give me 24 hours to prove to you how good a burglar I am. Whatever I steal, you can keep. Let me show you."

The challenge was accepted. Ike said, "Just to let you know, I don't need any nickel and dime items: whatever you steal has got to be big. So don't go getting yourself arrested or killed for nothing. But all right. Twenty-four hours. Let's see what you can do."

*   *   *

The two maids brought the platters of meats and vegetables to the 20-foot long dinner table. The vast dining room, decorated with imported William Morris wallpaper and three crystal chandeliers, was quickly filled with the smell of onions. One of the maids served Cornelius Augustus Hardwicke; the other served his wife of 44 years, Agatha Jane, at the other end of the table.

Cornelius Augustus, financier, philanthropist, and owner of the lucrative Hudson Valley railroad ate his food with disinterest. His only child, Joanna Rebecca, weighed heavily on his mind. She was on her Grand Tour, now in Canada, and had fallen in love with the owner of a fleet of successful fishing boats. "A fisherman!" Cornelius blustered.

Agatha Jane, white-haired and dowdy, said, "Now, Corny, dear, what did Dr. Eberhardt say about this? He said to relax—that this happens all the time. She's only 18. The next man she meets, she will also fall in love with and want to marry. She's at that age of constant infatuation. I went through it, too. This consternation on your part is what ails your stomach and keeps you awake at night. It's not healthy."

Agatha did not utter an understatement: in the four days since he'd received the letter from Joanna Rebecca, Cornelius had neither slept nor eaten very much. He was no longer the picture of a hale old man. Brown circles pooled around his grey eyes. Deep furrows creased his brow. Though still a formidable man, his clothing began to sag on his frame. "I don't recall raising a harlot. The impudent young lady will require a thrashing when she returns."

"Enough of that!" Agatha replied. "You'll do no such thing! When she returns, she'll be sorry for distressing you, and you'll forgive her!"

"She'll be sorry, all right. And across my knee, I'll forgive her."

Agatha sighed into her plate, "Eat your filet mignon. It's your favorite."

The two maids eavesdropped from behind the kitchen door. One of them, Martha, said, "And I thought all them plantation massas were crazy. These white folk here have millions, enough money to buy away their worries. But they fight like they don't have enough money to put food on the table. They should just let the child enjoy herself!"

The other woman, Marian, shook her head, "Sometimes I'm glad I'm poor."

*   *   *

The residents of The Five Points braced for imminent battle—the tension seemed to boil from the crevices between the cobblestones. Two of the street gangs, each over 700 strong, had been threatening to do battle. Earlier in the year, the same two gangs, The Dead Rabbits and The Whyos, fought each other for five days, and only stopped because of exhaustion. Neither side won. Twenty-six teenagers and nine young men died.

The new difficulties had arisen in the previous two weeks, when a shipment of silk was warehoused at the Pearl Street piers. The Whyos' best breaking-and-entering man had been caught by the police, trying to steal the valuable material. Later, that same night, four of The Dead Rabbits' best burglars made off with $6,500 worth of the commodity. The Whyos accused The Dead Rabbits of tipping off the coppers, since the Rabbits' leader, Wee Petey Daley, owned Police Superintendent Michael Connery. Considering the larger, more perverse symbiosis that connected The Dead Rabbits to the Tammany political machine and the police, The Whyos' allegations were not unfounded. Scuffles erupted. The Whyos then attempted to steal the silk from The

Rabbits' headquarters. Four of its members were bludgeoned to death during the attempt.

The Whyos enlisted the support of Terry Billings' Bowery Boys. The Boys, still smarting and in mourning over the death of The Butcher, gladly lent their support. The Roach Guard, ever-hateful of The Bowery Boys, sided with The Dead Rabbits. The battle lines were drawn. Everyone waited.

*   *   *

Flophouse owner, Mrs. Nora Mooney, checked the condition of her shotgun, should rioting break out overnight. At three in the morning, she locked the front door of her house, grabbed a candle, and retired to her room. On her dresser lay a daguerreotype of her late husband and an unopened letter from her son.

She changed into her dressing gown and sat at the head of her bed. She brought the candle closer. Gently tearing open the envelope, she adjusted her spectacles, and read the letter within:

Dearest Mum,

I am doing well at college. I anticipate, once again, getting strong grades. In the memory of my father, and for the pride it gives you, I pray I do not disappoint. I am aware of the sacrifices you made for my education, and I remember the way you and father protected me from the riff-raff of the neighborhood...

"He needs more money," Nora Mooney mumbled.

...however, my finances are still strapped. I planned on working as a proofreader in a local print shop, but the wages and conditions were intolerable. I dread asking you for more assistance, but it is, alas, unavoidable.

"'Tis always 'unavoidable', me little scholar," she said aloud.

I require forty dollars to pay my way through the end of the term. Come May, I will return and work off my debt by doing repairs and chores around the boarding house. Please, remember that I hate to put you through further hardship.

Mrs. Mooney smiled. "But it is unavoidable?"

But it is necessary. I think of you fondly in all my waking hours, and dream of seeing you in six weeks.

Your loving son,

Patrick Aloysius

Mrs. Mooney kissed the signature on the letter, folded it, and replaced it in the envelope.

"Forty dollars!" she said. Calculating quickly, she estimated she had seven dollars in the flour jar in the pantry. But where would the balance come from? She was proud of her Patrick Aloysius, and knew he was not squandering the money she'd already sent. And yet, forty dollars! The cost of education, as she'd been warned, was indeed exorbitant.

*   *   *

Martha knew Cornelius Hardwicke would fire her, if he caught her, but the temptation to sneak out of her maid's quarters to raid the liquor cabinet was too strong. For 13 years, she had crept through the house in the dead of night and helped herself to a few snifters of brandy. At first, the darkness of the cavernous ballroom haunted her. Over the years, though, familiarity eased away those apprehensions. And with Mr. and Mrs. Hardwicke asleep upstairs and down the hall—practically half a block away—Martha did not fear any human visitations either.

However, Martha had been caught once, eleven years earlier. Joanna Rebecca, then only seven years old, had slipped passed her nanny on Christmas Eve, and made her way downstairs. She hoped to find Father Christmas putting her presents under the tree. Instead, she discovered Martha, feet up on an ottoman, holding a snifter of brandy on her lap.

"Martha! Are you waiting for Father Christmas, too?" the child had asked.

Startled, Martha nearly spilled the drink. "Miss Hardwicke! Lord! You scared the life out of me, child."

The girl approached her, and asked, "Are you going to give him that drink?"

Martha nodded, "Yes'm, Miss Hardwicke. I reckon Father Christmas might get a bit of a chill on this cold night."

The child smiled, "That's nice of you. You're a nice lady, Martha."

"Thank you, Miss Hardwicke," Martha said. "But don't tell your daddy. You know how much he don't like to give nothing away."

Joanna made a face of disgust, "I know. He's an old poop." She sat down by Martha's feet. "Very well. It's our secret."

That secret had been kept for 11 years. And those 11 years put the inevitable lines on Martha's face, put a burning sensation in Cornelius Augustus Hardwicke's abdomen every morning, and changed little Joanna into Miss Joanna Rebecca Hardwicke, looking for a proper suitor in Canada.

*　　　　　　*　　　　　　*

Martine stood before 4 East 41st Street, the Hardwicke Mansion. Having ridden illegally on the Hudson Valley railroad, Martine, like the other tramps, knew about the Hardwicke fortune. In a way, Martine felt bad for what he was about to do: Cornelius Hardwicke had done much for the poor. But if Martine wanted to join Ike Croft's fence operation, and therefore disappear in its deep-reaching network, he had to pull off an impressive burglary.

Martine circled the ponderous neo-classical structure four times. A lone guard snoozed in an armchair at the front door; no one guarded the back. A cellar window looked particularly inviting.

*   *   *

The next morning, Ike found the front door to his haberdasher's shop ajar. "Damnation!" he exclaimed. He pulled his revolver from the inner pocket of his maroon jacket and slowly entered the establishment.

"Signore Croft!" Luigi shouted enthusiastically. "Bravo! Guardalo! Look here!" Luigi gestured frantically to the open door to the storeroom. "When it was five o'clock this morning, Signore Martin come here. I let him in. He walk in here and he leave this for you." Luigi handed over a blue velvet pouch.

"Jayzus!" Ike exclaimed, when he peeked inside.

"Is beautiful, no?" Luigi asked.

"Is beautiful, YES!" Ike replied. He pulled out each item with the flourish of a magician pulling objects out of his hat. First, a diamond pendant, then a large emerald brooch, strings of pearls, diamond earrings, sapphire tiepins, diamond rings, a gold bracelet embedded with rubies, a gold and diamond pocket watch, and, in its own velvet pouch, a silver pistol with a pearl handle. "Bloody beautiful!"

A note, at the bottom of the pouch, read, "Courtesy of Cornelius Hardwicke."

*   *   *

The crime was so extraordinary, so shocking, that Police Superintendent Michael Connery journeyed to the Hardwicke Mansion. He first interrogated the night watchman, but came away convinced that he had seen no one. The cook also saw no one, heard nothing.

The two maids were called to the master bedroom. The older one, Marian, told Connery, "At 10:30, me and Martha finished cleanin' the dining room and the kitchen. We went to our room, which is downstairs, sir, by the wine cellar. And we talked, and..."

"Talked about what?" Connery asked, massaging his heavy black mustache.

"O, netthin', really," Marian answered.

"Surely, ye must have spoke of something."

"Well, yes, sir," Marian began. "Only the usual things. Who was goin' to buy the groceries, do the laundry...you know, netthin' different."

"Nothing at all?" Connery asked.

Marian thought for a moment, and then said, "Well, now that I recollect...but it wasn't much of anything."

Thirty-three year-old Superintendent Connery had anticipated this. The tall, lanky Connery had been a lawman since the day after his 20th birthday. But, as the 1850s drew to a close, he had become repulsed by the overwhelming corruption and inefficiency of the Municipals. It came as no surprise to Connery, then, that the Republican Governor King would impose his own police force—the Metropolitans—upon the City. When that happened, Connery had shrewdly played both ends against the middle; while remaining outwardly friendly and sympathetic to City Hall, Tammany Hall and the local Irish who supported the Municipals, Connery secretly worked against them by informing for the Metropolitans. When the dust settled after the Police Riots in the summer of '57, Connery's appointment to the upper echelons of the new police department pleased the upstate Republicans who privately acknowledged his help, and placated the disposition of the local Irish population who were glad to see one of their own succeed.

However, Connery could not foresee the two things that would later plague him: first, the Metropolitans were slowly but surely falling under the powerful influences of Tammany Hall and its rising star, William Magear Tweed; and, second, it put him under the close scrutiny of the Nativist, Know-Nothing Party which fiercely fought anything which was not White—Anglo-Saxon—Protestant.

As New York City's first Irish Catholic Superintendent of Police, he often felt that he had something to prove. He had solved many of the city's most sensational cases with celerity, using every interrogation technique—legal or not—that he knew. Those successes, combined with the steep tributes he'd paid to the Tweed machine, facilitated his rapid climb through the ranks.

Over the years, he'd come to know that what a witness often considered nothing was actually of great significance. He felt intuitively that the slow-moving and apparently kind-souled Marian had not committed the crime. However, twitchy, bleary-eyed Martha seemed to be holding something back. She sat restlessly beneath the portrait of young Joanna Rebecca Hardwicke. "What is that ye spoke of, Marian?" Connery asked.

"Miss Joanna, sir."

"Joanna Hardwicke?"

"Yes," Marian said. "Miss Joanna is in love with a fisherman, somewhere in Canada. Master Hardwicke was in a fury about that."

"Please continue, Marian."

Marian turned to Martha, then back to Superintendent Connery. "Well, Martha was a bit upset about it. Martha, bein' closer to the child than I ever was, didn't want to see netthin' bad happen to her. She said something about a Christmas Eve long ago they'd spent together. I can't really recollect exactly. To be honest, sir, I was too tired to be payin' it much mind. I work very hard."

Connery nodded his head. "I understand, Marian. And I hope ye don't think I wished to trouble ye. It's me job."

"Yes, sir."

"Ye can go, now." Connery said. And Marian, as quickly as she could, left.

Connery placed his hand on Martha's quivering knee. "Are ye feelin' well, Martha?"

"Yes, sir," Martha replied. But Martha was not feeling well at all. Before her, the bodies of Cornelius Augustus and Agatha Jane Hardwicke lay in their beds, each stabbed to death through the heart. They were being inspected by police and drawn by illustrators for the press. Martha fought an urge to vomit. She did not know whether or not Connery would believe the truth about what she had seen the night before. What white man would believe a black woman—a poor black woman in a rich white man's house—about what she'd witnessed?

*   *   *

Eddies of wind swirled pieces of trash along the cobblestones and walkways. Mrs. Nora Mooney tried to sweep the area in front of her flophouse clean, but the garbage was ultimately blown back. She mused, "Why couldn't this be money? It just keeps returnin'." She smiled sadly.

"Good morning, Mrs. Mooney," Martine said.

Mrs. Mooney looked up through her spectacles. "Good morning to ye, Mr. Martin. How ye be?"

Martine ran his fingers through his dark hair. "Fine," he replied. "Windy day."

"That it is," the old widow nodded. She leaned on her broom. "Have ye found yerself a place?"

"Yes, on Cherry Street," Martine answered.

Mrs. Mooney shrugged. "Tis all alike in this neighborhood. Be careful."

"I am," Martine said. "Be careful yourself, Mrs. Mooney."

Waving a hand, she laughed. "Nobody bothers an old woman whose son is sending her to the almshouse."

Martine assumed that the frumpy flophouse owner was referring to the costs of bail money. "How's that?" he asked.

"He's in college. Rutgers. He wants to be a doctor." She smiled proudly. "The lad is smart as a whip."

"I'd wager he is," Martine said. "He must get it from his mother who's smart enough to run her own business."

"O, Mr. Martin! Ye flatter me!" she exclaimed, blushing. Then she sighed deeply. "But the *cost!* Forty dollars, just to get him to the end of the term! Where will the money come from?" Mrs. Mooney answered her own question, "I shall have to pawn my wedding ring."

Martine smiled. "No," he said. He reached into his pocket, where he had Cornelius Hardwicke's money clip. "Here," he said, handing the old woman four ten dollar bills. "Pay me when you have the money."

Old Nora, stunned, examined the bills. "Sir? Thank…" But the years reminded her of what kind of men so easily make such loans. "Hold on. What's the interest?"

Martine laughed. "None." He added, "Can't a man help a struggling young student? Good day, Mrs. Mooney." He bowed and walked away proud. Very proud. Proud of Mrs. Mooney for supporting her son. How could Martine ever have entertained the idea of murdering her? He was proud of young Master Mooney for getting out of the neighborhood, and bettering himself. And, of course, Martine was proud of Martine. He was a bad man and he knew it. But, for once, the demons weren't dominating him, although they had the previous night—but that was an extraordinary circumstance. "Perhaps," he mused, "I am surrounded by so many human demons here, that the ones that torment me are no longer needed."

*　　　　　*　　　　　*

"These are very good pieces, Ike," Gerald "Kid Gas" Gasser commented, as he held the stolen jewelry up to the light. "Very nice, very clean." He put down the ruby-studded gold bracelet, and then scratched away furiously at the eczema that was eating away at the skin on his forearms. "These are top-dollar items, I can tell you."

Confidently twirling the end of his curly grey mustache, Ike Croft just hmmed in acknowledgment. Although Ike was a good fence in his own right, there were some items, the high-priced items, that he knew he would have difficulty selling to the residents of The Five Points. He could sell stolen coats, boots, liquor, and so on, to the gangs or to some of the more successful thieves in the neighborhood, but these priceless gems were beyond the scope of his network. In these circumstances, he turned to Kid Gas.

Nineteen year old Kid Gas had been a fence for seven years under the tutelage of his Aunt Freida, whose used furniture store was a front for the city's largest fencing operation, moving over two million dollars in stolen merchandise a year. Kid Gas, blue-eyed and pink-skinned, looked like a kid, but was taught by his aunt to act adult, and, more importantly, to treat his clients as adults. "Never try to cheat, never try to gyp: give them a fair price that makes them satisfied, but will also turn a profit for you. If you do anything less than that," she had warned, "you will only deal in cheap merchandise, have unhappy customers or, worse, wind up with a bullet in your back." Kid Gas obeyed his tiny aunt, and earned very good money for a man his age. Although Ike was, at best, an inconsistent client—sometimes he had good merchandise, sometimes not—Kid Gas always gave him a good price. "I'll take it all, except for the pocket watch and the pistol. Two thousand."

Ike was happy with the price—he'd only expected fifteen hundred—but asked, "Out of curiosity, lad, what's wrong with the watch and gun?"

"Nothing's wrong with the quality of them," Kid answered. "But they are monogrammed. They're easily identifiable, and I'll have no part of it. Should you scratch off those initials, you damage the goods." Then Kid Gas asked, "You say these came from the Hardwicke estate?"

Ike replied, "Aye."

Somewhat impressed, Kid said, "You got yourself a brave little thief, there. My best advice is to sell the watch and gun at any price you can. Just get them off your property before the coppers find them."

Late as usual, Francis "Hungry Frank" Hughes entered the shop. He was reading the morning edition of *The World*. Hungry Frank was skeletal no matter how much he ate. His frame was an advantage to his burglary and breaking-and-entering career, as it permitted him to squeeze between iron bars and slide down the narrowest chimneys. He waved the newspaper over his head, and announced, "This gentleman must be mad! Did ye hear about the Hardwicke job?"

Kid Gas smiled at Ike. Ike looked at Hungry Frank, who was dressed in an orange and brown, ill-fitting waistcoat. He asked, "What's wrong with pinching quality stuff?"

"Absolutely nothing!" Hungry Frank responded. "I give credit to the man. But why spoil it?"

"What do you mean 'spoil it'?" Kid Gas asked.

"Well," Hungry Frank explained, "why successfully sneak into a mansion, pinch what ye want, and then murder the family in their beds for no reason?"

"What!?" Ike roared. The pickled herring he'd had at Abie's seemed to explode in his stomach. "Who was murdered?"

"Mr. and Mrs. Hardwicke...in their beds. Once through the heart with a short-bladed knife!" Hungry Frank said. "Didn't ye hear? It's all over the streets! The coppers are hot to catch this madman! Tis the crime of the century, next to the Jewett and Burdell cases."

Kid Gas shook his head. "Sorry, Ike. These items are too dangerous. The price has just gone down: one thousand-three hundred is my only offer."

*   *   *

Luigi returned home at eight in the morning, bringing with him four loaves of bread. He lived with his wife, his two sons, his younger brother, his nephew, and his mother-in-law in a two-bedroom apartment on Mulberry Bend. Wearily, yet, content, he entered the apartment. The family spoke in fast-paced Sicilian. "Good morning, everybody! I got some bread!" Luigi announced.

His two young boys, Mario, 4, and Antonio, 2, each hugged one of their father's legs. "Papa! Papa!" they cried in joy.

The other men of the household had departed for their menial jobs. They all worked hard, pooling their money to pay the rent, and, eventually, bring over more relatives from the dreadfully impoverished mountains of Sicily.

Luigi's wife, Maria, 18, greeted him indifferently, but he could detect a sort of sorrow, or sickness, in her deep-set, dark eyes. "What's the matter? You don't like the bread?" he asked.

Luigi's mother-in-law, frail with pursed wrinkled lips, shook her head, as she peeled potatoes over the sink.

"The bread is fine," Maria said softly. "I was sick this morning, that's all."

But that wasn't all. Luigi knew she was pregnant. He sighed at the prospect of a new expense. "Well, Maria," he said, "I'm sure Signore Croft will help us."

Maria dropped the bread on the wooden table and ran sobbing to the bedroom. Little Antonio, seeing his mother so distressed, began to cry, as well.

"Now, what did I say?" Luigi asked in exasperation.

All his mother-in-law muttered was, "Stupido!"

*   *   *

After eating a light breakfast, Martine returned to his one-room apartment. He hadn't slept in 28 hours, and he hoped the food in his stomach would be conducive to sleep. He'd earlier considered having a big breakfast, but the mere thought of it made him gag.

Wearily, he closed the dingy curtains and rubbed his eyes. He undressed and lay upon the stained mattress on the bed. Almost immediately, he dozed into a deep, dreamless sleep.

But it did not last.

The ghouls surrounded his bed, filled his room. Some were bloodied, some were eviscerated, some gigantic, some dwarfish. Most were human, others birdlike. They didn't speak to him, as such, but he knew what was being communicated. The ghoul at his feet rattled the bed frame. It appeared to be feminine, but the blood and gore on its visage precluded any positive identification. It summoned him to wake. *Rattle! Rattle! Awake!*

Looking down upon himself, Martine perceived something crawling about under his skin, in his chest cavity. It coiled itself tightly around his heart and then let go: coil and release, coil and release, coil and release. Then faster and tighter: *coilrelease, coilrelease, coilrelease, coilrelease.* Martine grabbed at the pain in his chest, dug under his skin with his fingernails, and extracted the snakelike creature. Everything went black.

When the light returned, Martine found himself standing naked on a muddy road in the countryside. His blood dripped from the newly created wound on his chest. Before him was a small, wood frame house. He was compelled to knock on the door. The woman, not quite thirty, not quite pretty, red-haired and tiny, screamed when he entered. "Why are you screaming?" he asked.

But the woman did not respond. She backed up into the house. Under each arm, she guarded her young sons. "Don't scream," he pleaded. "Don't be afraid."

"Mama!" one of the boys cried. "Who is this man?"

"DONG!" the grandfather clock exclaimed. "DONG! DEATH! DONG! DEATH!"

"This is a nice home. I like Dobbs Ferry, " Martine said. "So why are you screaming?"

But the woman did not scream anymore. The upper right portion of her skull had been chopped out by the axe in Martine's hand. "I'm sorry," Martine said. "Forgive me."

Martine then saw one of her sons fall to the floor. He saw the blade of his axe slice away the front of the boy's throat. The child lay by his mother's corpse. He grabbed at his collar, twitching, twitching, twitching, the blood spilling, spilling.

"Come back!" Martine hollered to the other boy. "Please, I'm sorry I forgot to feed the cows!"

The boy, attempting to escape through the back door, did not take his eyes off Martine.

"DONG! DEATH! DONG! DEATH!"

The boy ran squarely into the wall next to the back door. He fell.

"I'm sorry!" Martine cried. He saw the axe split open the middle of the boy's face. "Stop it!" Martine said to the axe. "Stop it!" The axe came down on the boy's collarbone, and then, deeply, into his chest. "O, forgive me, forgive me, forgive me, forgive me..."

*   *   *

While Superintendent Connery continued his investigation at the Hardwicke Mansion, he ordered Martha carted downtown to Police Headquarters. She sat between two officers in a covered police wagon. She had not said much to Connery at the mansion, except to deny that she had committed the heinous crime.

"Ye know, John," the red-bearded officer began, "Mr. Hardwicke donated quite a bit of money to the Policeman's Fund."

The other officer, John, who sported black mutton-chop sideburns, replied, "Aye. He did. But now no more."

"Imagine! Killed in their beds by a bloody nigger."

John nodded, "Tis horrible."

The pony and cart clip-clopped down Fifth Avenue. Shoppers and pedestrians milled about the department stores, in spite of the impending rain. Martha peered anxiously through the bars on the door. She had not been this far downtown in years.

The red-bearded officer continued, "Now, if I had the fortune to catch the murderer of the Hardwickes, ye know what I'd do, John?"

"What's that, then?" John asked.

The officer gripped his nightstick and bashed Martha across the temple. "That's what I'd do."

"Don't hit the prisoner," John said disinterestedly.

"I was just demonstrating what I *would* do, if I had the murderer here. Ye know I would probably do this too..." he raised the nightstick again.

Blood dripping from over her ear, Martha exclaimed, "I ain't no killer, sir. Please don't hit me."

"If yer not the killer," the red-bearded officer began, "then why did the Superintendent have us take ye downtown?"

Martha, still eyeing the raised club, replied, "I don't rightly know, sir. He thinks I know who done it."

"Well, I think I know who done it, too," he replied. "Ye stink of liquor. I think that last night ye got into the old man's whiskey, he caught ye and fired ye. Then ye went to the kitchen, grabbed a knife, went upstairs and killed him. Since the old woman was a witness, ye had to kill her, too. That's what ye done!" He brought the nightstick down on Martha's knee.

John repeated, "Don't hit the prisoner."

"Aww..." Martha groaned, wrapping her arms around her lap. She cried, "If you did have the murderer here, he'd take that damned stick out of your hands and make you swallow it! He was The Devil himself! I seen him! I seen him! The Devil walks the Earth!"

✶   ✶   ✶

Mrs. Mooney sipped a cup of tea in the kitchen of her flophouse. She smoothed a piece of paper on the top of the table, and began writing:

Dear son,

I am glad your schooling is good, and I know that you will get high grades.

You will find in this letter the $40 that you need. I got it from a gentleman named Mr. Martin, who lent it to me free of interest. Remember him in your prayers for what he's done.

You know I do not like to write much, so I'll say goodbye. Be good. I love you.

Your mother

Finishing her tea, Nora Mooney sealed the envelope and decided she would walk directly to the Post Office in spite of the rain outside. A loving parent does no less.

*   *   *

At two in the afternoon, Petey Daley, leader of The Dead Rabbits, entered Ike Croft's Haberdashers. Standing impatiently in the middle of Ike's shop, he called out, "Come, now, ye old sot! I haven't much time!"

Ike barreled out of the "office". Petey could tell that the smile on Ike's face was forced. "Mr. Daley, I'm glad ye made it."

The two men shook hands. "Ye summoned me and I came. Ye have something of interest, I imagine."

Ike nodded. "Indeed, son. Come with me." Petey followed the middle-aged haberdasher into the storeroom. Petey Daley had been there several times before, and Ike usually had something that tickled Petey's fancy.

Ike grabbed the blue velvet pouch, and showed him the Hardwicke pistol and pocket watch that Kid Gas would not buy. "Aren't they lovely?" he asked.

"I'll say," Petey agreed. He inspected the pearl-handled revolver. "Lovely, indeed." He then took the pocket watch, clipped the chain to a shirt button, and dropped the watch into his pocket. "Jolly good."

"One hundred dollars for both," Ike said.

"Fifty," Petey offered.

"Fifty? O, Mr. Daley...it's pure silver, perfect diamonds, perfect pearl..."

Petey placed the barrel of the pistol against the bridge of Ike's nose. "Maybe ye want a perfect hole between those beady eyes of yers. Fifty, I said."

Ike smiled nervously, "That is a generous offer, Mr. Daley. I accept."

Petey withdrew the weapon and placed it in his waistband. "Done!" Petey said.

As Petey paid Ike, Martine limped into the storeroom: the dampness caused severe soreness in his knee. Petey whipped out the pistol and aimed it at Martine.

"No!" Ike shouted. "He's one of mine."

Petey, once again, stuck the gun in the waistband of his trousers. "Tell me, Ike, do ye let all yer people just prance in here? Although with that bugger's limp, it could hardly be called prancin'."

"I'm sorry for the interruption, Mr. Daley. Excuse me." Ike walked over to Martine. "Where have you been? Christ, man, are you mad? Wait for me outside."

Martine shrugged and left the storeroom.

But Petey Daley followed him. He was curious about the new man on the scene. "Sir, wait!" Petey called out, pushing past Ike and into the shop proper.

Martine turned. "Yes."

"Yer new around here," Petey noted.

"Yes, sir, I am," Martine responded. "A few days."

Petey nodded. "Only a few days and Old Ike's already hired ye?"

"Yes, sir."

Petey scratched his scalp, "I imagine ye have some special talent. Otherwise, Old Ike wouldn't bother with ye. Am I right?"

Martine looked over to Ike, who listened to the exchange with concern. Then he answered, "Sir, I don't know who you are, so, please, take no offense—but what I do for Mr. Croft is between him and me. Understand?"

Ike cringed.

But Wee Petey just smiled. "Yes, I understand, and no offense taken. And I wouldn't dream of interfering with Ike's business. But remember my name: Petey Daley. Should ye need extra work, come see me."

Martine DelaCroix extended his hand. "My name's Mr. Martin. Pleased to meet you."

"Very well, then, Mr. Martin." The two shook hands. Petey then saluted Ike: "A pleasure doin' business with ye, friend." He then left the shop and hurried back to The Dead Rabbits' Headquarters.

Ike wiped the sweat that dripped from under his grey hair. He walked over to Martine. "You must be charmed. Nobody tells Petey Daley that somethin' isn't his business."

Martine shrugged. "I judged him to be a decent man."

Ike informed Martine, "Mr. Daley is the leader of The Dead Rabbits: the most vicious gang in this area. He practically rules the Bloody Sixth Ward! Between the loyalty of his boys and the fact that he's got the Police Superintendent in his pocket, Petey Daley not only gets away with murder, he thrives on it."

"Oh," Martine said. "I see."

"Yes, you certainly must be charmed. Or mad," Ike said. And for the first time, Ike realized he might need to fear Martine, whether he was charmed or mad. "Lad, I must ask you something:

why did you kill the old couple—the Hardwickes? The price of yer goods dropped because they're dangerous: evidence in a murder."

"They saw me," Martine answered. "I had to."

"In their beds?"

"No," Martine replied. "I put them in their beds after they surprised me. I wanted it to appear that one of the servants did it. Or some lunatic." Martine had no qualms about lying to his employer. He quickly remembered how, after he had snatched what he wanted, the ghouls put his three-inch dagger in his hands and forced him to kill the Hardwickes in their sleep. "I had to," he repeated.

"Ah!" Ike exclaimed, somewhat relieved. "Nonetheless," he reached into his pocket, "here's two hundred dollars. You earned it."

Martine shook his head. "No, Ike, it's yours. All you owe me is work. Am I on?"

Ike smiled and popped Martine on the shoulder. "Yes, Martine, that you are!"

Martine began to smile. But in the corner of his eye he saw a battered, bloody specter, draped in a black death shroud. Its eye sockets were hollow; its head noseless and earless. Through cracked teeth it hissed, "Kill!"

Martine blurted, "I must leave now."

"Leave?" Ike asked. "Where to? Come, lad, let's have a drink together at The Suicide Hall!"

The apparition, formidable and angry, drifted toward Ike. A small, skeletal hand emerged from one of the ghoul's gory eye sockets and reached for the middle-aged haberdasher.

Martine spun around. "I can't. Good-day, Mr. Croft."

Ike watched the muscular little man hurry out of the shop. He noted the sweat on the back of Martine's collar. "Queer fellow," he muttered. He patted the money in his trouser pocket.

*   *   *

Old Hermann Graebel took pride in his thirty-eight years as caretaker of Potter's Field. In fact, he would often introduce himself by announcing, "I'm Hermann Graebel, the caretaker of Potter's Field," whenever he made a rare trip away from Hart's Island. The tall, haggard old man's pride was not unfounded. In the decades he'd served as caretaker, he oversaw the burial of just about every corpse that had been interred by the leg-shackled convicts who were ferried in daily from Bedloe's Island. Frequently, he'd buried people with his own coarse hands and strong back.

Except for the grey sprouts of hair from his ears and a queer, pinwheel-like spray of brownish-white hair just above his forehead, Hermann was nearly hairless: thin, white eyebrows; short, pale eyelashes; no facial hair. His taut, lightly creased skin and severe cheekbones exaggerated the depth of the sockets around his pale blue eyes. In fact, Hermann was pleased that he very much looked like a Gothic-novel caricature of the people he respected most: the dead.

To him, Death was neither a simple dimming of life's lantern nor was it the entrance to a Christian or heathen afterworld. Hermann enjoyed the metaphor that Death was the final page of a book: a book could not be deemed "good" or "bad" until it was finished, just as a painting could not be called "beautiful" until the last stroke of color was applied. Therefore, a life could not be judged "full" or "depraved", "good" or "wicked" until it was over, for a wicked man could be redeemed, and a good one corrupted. Few men understood Death better than Hermann Graebel. Few people understood life better than Hermann Graebel.

After nailing down a loose shingle on the roof of his shack, Hermann prepared to climb down his ladder when he saw Officer J.D. Cavanaugh steer the death-cart through the main gate to the graveyard. Officer Cavanaugh waved. Hermann responded in kind. He climbed down the ladder, wiped his hands on his trousers, and approached the cart.

"Afternoon, Hermann," the red-haired officer said.

"Good afternoon, my friend," the old caretaker replied. He stepped to the back of the greyish-brown cart and lifted the brown burlap covering. A swarm of flies buzzed away from the disturbance. Hermann observed the bodies of eight children burned and blackened so badly that their sex could not be determined. "Ach," Hermann sighed, "children." He shook his head.

"Catholic orphanage was burned, two nights ago," Officer Cavanaugh informed his friend. "We think the bloody Know-Nothings done it, but there's no proof—and probably never will be."

"Yes, but who else would commit such an act?" Hermann asked rhetorically. "Why were they brought here?"

Barely able to look at the tiny corpses without gagging, the young officer replied, "Records were burned. Dozens of other babies ran through the streets in the night—no telling who these are!"

"Ach," Hermann said. "And who is this?" he asked, pointing to the body at the back of the cart. The open-eyed corpse was that of a large, teenaged boy. His head had been twisted so badly, he seemed to peer from over his shoulder blades. His neck was distorted to a violent purple.

Officer Cavanaugh, glad to have his attention drawn away from the corpses of the children, said, "A thug from The Five Points. No one there knew his name or his family, if he had any. All they knew was that he was trouble: a brawler, thief. Fact is, the people said they were glad to be rid of him." Scratching his curly red beard, he added, "Doesn't seem right that he's on the cart with the young ones."

"Nothing on this cart can be called old or young, anymore." Hermann pulled on his fingerless work gloves. "And certainly nothing on this cart can be judged right or wrong either, eh, my friend?"

*   *   *

From Cornelius Hardwicke's valet, Superintendent Connery obtained a list of the items that had been stolen from the murdered tycoon: a pearl-handled revolver, a diamond pocket watch, four gold rings, and two sapphire tie-pins. Several items had also been stolen from Agatha Jane's jewelry chest. As Connery and his men rode in a covered pony and trap, the Superintendent looked through his notes:

Entry made by perpetrator through broken window near wine cellar at rear of house.

Perpetrator did not know house well: several opened doors in upper hallway indicate he was searching for master bedroom.

Perpetrator brought his own murder weapon—no cutlery missing from kitchen.

Victims killed in sleep.

Perpetrator killed Agatha Jane first: trail of her blood leads from her bed to her husband's.

Coroner: 'Perpetrator was strong, muscular. Knife thrusts were deep. Bruises around wounds indicate that the hilt of the knife hit skin.'

Connery folded his notes and put them into his breast pocket. As he twirled the end of his bushy mustache, he muttered, "Either

I have a madman who's tryin' to pass himself off as a burglar or a burglar who's posin' as a madman. Bloody Hell."

A heavy-set officer asked, "Who do you think did it, sir?"

Connery shook his head.

"Well, do you think it was one of the maids?"

"Nay," Connery said. "Twas a male, and an outsider. What maid would kill her employer and his wife, and then go back to bed knowin' she'd be caught by us in the mornin'?"

"A smart maid hoping a copper would think just like the way you just did?" the pudgy officer asked.

The Superintendent clucked his tongue against the roof of his mouth. "Perhaps. But I'll say this: those women didn't seem particularly smart or criminal. They were just loyal. And ye don't find much loyalty around these days."

As he scratched his paunch, the officer asked, "So why did you have the one maid brought downtown?"

Connery ceased toying with the brush on his upper lip. "Did ye see the look on her face, lad? That was sheer fright! Not fear of incarceration or the gallows. That poor woman had been gripped by a Holy Terror! She saw *something*, and I'm goin' to find out what that was."

The officer shrugged. "I couldn't tell much. All them Negroes look the same to me, no matter what they're thinking or feeling."

"Lad," Connery said, jabbing the gut of the officer with his forefinger, "that's why you'll never be anything more than a regular street copper. That woman could have been as blue as me uniform, but it was in her eyes that ye had to look. Fear cannot be hid behind eyelids, no matter what color they be."

*　　　　*　　　　*

High Collar Browne, leader of The Whyos (who earned his nickname from his penchant for oversized paper shirt collars), conferred with his ally, the long-legged Terry Billings, leader of The Bowery Boys. The two young men, and several of their confederates, huddled around a dilapidated billiard table in the cellar of The Whyos headquarters. A single kerosene lantern, suspended from the ceiling, cast a garish light.

Green-eyed High Collar tilted his dirty stovepipe hat to one side. "We fight the little Catholic bastards tonight," he announced. "That much is certain."

A hare-lipped young boy listened attentively to the discussion.

"We have them outnumbered?" Terry Billings asked. "Even if The Roach Guard joined with them?"

"Yes, we do. Don't we, split-lip?" High Collar asked the hare-lipped boy. The boy did not respond. High Collar turned back to Terry Billings. "They have close to 1,400. We got over 1,600 combined, more or less. Anyway, we go after them at supper-time and catch them off-guard"

"Aye," Terry said, "but Wee Petey has hired that blasted Black Roger. He can fight like a dozen men."

High Collar shrugged, "We can still get Chickie Boone. The boy is as strong as an ox."

Terry shook his head. "Nay. The boy is not trustworthy. I had to break his ribs once fer botchin' a simple job, a while back. Forget him."

"Fine," the leader of The Whyos muttered. He ran a lanky finger under his collar. "We target Black Roger first. Once he's taken care of, we go for the rest."

"Done," Terry Billings said. He stood up, scratched his crotch, and stretched his long legs. "We go just after sundown and attack The Rabbits' headquarters. We take two teams: one up Orange

Street, the other up Cross. We'll trap that little shite Petey Daley in a vise. He's as good as buried."

The hare-lipped young boy slipped out the back door.

*   *   *

Martine stood before the locked door to Mrs. Mooney's flop-house. He gathered the collar of his pea green waistcoat to his throat. The fierce winds and rain battered him. Drops rolled down the smooth skin of his face.

Martine was afraid; it wasn't unusual for the ghouls to appear when Martine was lying in his bed. But they never dared to appear in broad daylight, out in the streets. The schoolteacher in Suffern, the family in Dobbs Ferry, the Hardwickes...they were all killed under orders from the demons in the dead of night. But now they materialized in mid-morning or mid-afternoon. Out in the streets, the apparitions were not as brazen as the one that appeared in Ike Croft's haberdasher's shop, but they were there, lurking in the periphery of his vision: in muddy alleyways, behind dark tene-ment windows, behind piles of offal. Martine often wished them away. Once he prayed for them to leave him alone, but that only caused them to mock him all the more. He needed the matronly Mrs. Mooney. Nora Mooney, the goodness in her being, kept the demons away.

In the torrential downpour, Martine could barely see across the street. Images scampered through the swirling mists. Others stood staring at him, until he looked back, and, then, they vanished. Martine stifled an urge to cry. The storm clouds held back nothing.

*   *   *

In spite of his mother-in-law's evaluation, Luigi was not a stu-pid man; he was a naive one. If a person who'd spent his entire life in The Five Points were to trust someone else from The Five Points, he would be considered stupid. But for a recent immigrant from Italy to trust someone in The Five Points, one can only fairly assess him or her as naive. And Luigi trusted Ike Croft.

At dusk, Luigi awakened. He peered out the cracked window. The rain had stopped. The gas lamps were lit. In the streets below, the shopkeepers hurriedly shut their stores, and trotted home before the garrotters would begin their prowls. Stray dogs and pigs lapped at puddles in the muddy street.

Luigi stepped into his trousers and pulled the suspenders over his shoulders. He threw on a stained shirt and a black vest. He quietly stepped over his sleeping younger brother and nephew; they had just finished putting in 14 hours stuffing and stitching mattresses.

When he entered the kitchen, there was a plate of boiled potatoes and string beans in tomato sauce waiting for him. Maria sat with her hands folded on her lap. "Eat," she said in a Sicilian dialect. Her mother was knitting feverishly in the corner of the room. The two little boys slept at their grandmother's feet.

Luigi greedily devoured the food. When he was done, he asked, "Are you still upset?"

"No," Maria answered. "I was this morning. I'm sorry." She looked at her hands. "Luigi, we must talk about this."

Luigi agreed. "Yes. But everything will be fine."

"I hope," Maria replied.

"I know!" Luigi asserted. He grabbed his short-brimmed hat. Leaning over to his beautiful young wife, he kissed Maria on the forehead. "I love you, Maria. I must go now. Do you need anything for tomorrow?"

"No," Maria answered. "Be careful."

"I will, " Luigi replied. He called out to his mother-in-law, "Supper was delicious!"

She responded with, "Go to work."

Luigi shook his head and sighed. He kissed his wife again, and headed out the door.

"Stupido," Maria's mother grumled

"Mama!" Maria shouted.

               *   *   *

Zachary ("Old Zack") Pembroke Farragut, Manhattan District Attorney, sat in Police Superintendent Connery's office, as he anxiously awaited the arrival of the beleaguered law enforcement official. This meeting would be important. The late Cornelius Hardwicke had been a great benefactor to Tammany Hall and Old Zack was under pressure from it: whoever killed the Hardwickes had to be found and punished.

Although Old Zack had managed to so far keep himself out of Tammany's corrupt grip, he did acknowledge its power, and Tammany needed to keep someone of Zack's integrity and popularity in the forefront of the public's attention.

Old Zack, thin, bespectacled, with wisps of white hair behind each ear, had reached the ripe old age of 76. He had lived through and seen it all in New York City, including the sensational murders of Helen Jewett and Dr. Harvey Burdell, and the Police Riots. Depending on the nature of the case, Zachary had either worked closely with Superintendent Connery or butted heads with him. But even when they were adversaries, they had respected each other's positions and learned from the experience.

Old Zack knew the Superintendent well. He knew that Connery was a methodical and thorough investigator who neither tolerated the ignorance of his inferiors nor disobeyed the wishes of those above him—no matter how much he may have vehemently disagreed with them.

When it came to Connery's involvement with The Five Points gangs, however, Old Zack's respect turned to pity. In The Five Points, Connery's men were outnumbered and out armed by the various gangs, especially Petey Daley and his Dead Rabbits. But there was a much more pertinent equation which created this stalemate between the police and the gangs: Tammany Hall needed the gangs to intimidate voters in the Irish and free Black districts to vote Democrat; the gangs needed the police to stay away from their operations; and police officials like Connery needed to pay Tammany Hall for continued advancement and job security. For any one party to betray or revolt against another would be to jeopardize its own survival. Although District Attorney Farragut had the power to expose this cycle, he was reluctant to do so.

Perhaps an explanation for Zachary Farragut's desire to turn his back on Connery's involvement with The Dead Rabbits would be found in something he'd once told the press in an unrelated incident: "If a public official does nine good deeds for New York City, but does only one bad, that is more than I have a right to expect from him; for, these days, it seems that so many officials do nine bad deeds and only one good one, and yet still expect a statue dedicated to them on the lawn of City Hall."

Looking tired and with two sheets to the wind, Superintendent Connery entered his office. "I can't say I'm surprised to see ye, Zack," he said. After tossing an armload of paperwork onto his desk, he pulled out his chair and sat. "How be ye?"

Old Zack rose slowly from his hardback chair. "Just a bit of the rheumatism that comes with old age, Mike. Nothing much else, fortunately. Any news on the Hardwicke case?"

Connery sighed loudly. He licked his heavy black mustache. "The boys upstairs are a bit nervous, are they?" He opened a desk drawer and pulled out a bottle of whiskey. "Are ye thirsty, old friend?" he asked, as he took two shot glasses from out of the drawer. "Please, sit."

"Thank you, I will," Zachary replied. "A small whiskey will do."

As he poured, Connery asked, "Are the higher ups in Tammany and City Hall squeezing ye on this Hardwicke case?"

Zack sipped. "They're squeezing me harder than I care to describe. They want this killer badly, Mike. They want to ease the public's concern. After all, if someone like Cornelius Hardwicke can be murdered in his own home, how safe are any of our citizens..."

"Stop the malarkey, Zack. It doesn't become ye," Connery said. "The gods in Tammany are afraid that something is underfoot and out to get them." He put down his shot glass. "Am I right?"

Zack exhaled deeply. "Yes, Mike," he said. He sipped his whiskey. "Well, do you think that this is the case? Was Hardwicke killed as part of a conspiracy to get to Tammany?"

"I don't believe so," Connery replied. "And I'll have a better idea once I speak to the witness."

"The maid?"

"Aye," the Superintendent answered. "One Martha Adams."

Zack leaned forward in his seat. "Let me ask you, Mike, because you know they will ask me: why do you think that this was a random killing, and not a direct attack on Hardwicke?"

Connery waved his forefinger before his face. "Nay! I never said that this was a random killin'. The Hardwickes were selected, and then deliberately executed."

"You've lost me, Mike."

Connery nodded, acknowledging the confusing start to his thesis. "I'm sorry. I'll start over. Let's say the worst is true: there's someone out there that Tammany and Billy Tweed crossed—or his Ring crossed—and now he or they are lookin' to strike back. And they chose to start with the Hardwickes."

"Go on," the old prosecutor requested.

"Now, think," the Superintendent continued, "who was the most vulnerable member of that family?"

"I don't know."

"Miss Joanna Hardwicke! All alone, over in Europe! Now in Canada," Connery exclaimed. "Ye send a thug over there or up to Toronto, have her kidnapped, and Old Corny would pay any price because he loves his daughter so much—and he may have something in his closet that he wishes to keep there."

"Like the fact he contributed hundreds of thousands of dollars to Tammany and Tweed," Old Zack offered.

"Aye! So let's keep on this track. Now, imagine that fer some reason they couldn't get to the lass—or that they didn't want money, they wanted blood. Why kill the old woman, Agatha? It would just fuel the flames of public outrage—as they are right now. The papers are crying fer justice, and that isn't good fer those involved."

Zack suggested the obvious, "They killed her because she was a witness."

Connery smiled, "Aye. And short of havin' to kill her, how do ye prevent her from bein' a witness?"

Old Zack's eyes widened behind his spectacles. "You kill Cornelius when Agatha —or anyone else, for that matter—is not around."

Connery thumped the top of his desk with his forefinger, "Aye! And that is the reason why I believe that this was not a murder specifically designed to assassinate Cornelius Hardwicke in order to gain revenge against Tammany."

The prosecutor nodded, but his forehead creased, "I understand that much now, but earlier you said that this was not a random killing. Now you're saying it's not a specific assassination. How…"

Connery held up his hand. "How can I justify both positions? Quite simply: This was not a deliberate attack on Cornelius Hardwicke, friend of Tammany Hall. This was a premeditated murder of Cornelius Hardwicke, The Very Wealthy Man. See the difference?" Enumerating the facts on his fingertips, Connery explained, "First, we know it's premeditated because the killer knew Hardwicke was wealthy and had something to steal. Second, it was premeditated because he brought his own weapon. And third, he killed the Hardwickes in their sleep—they could not be allowed to live."

"So, what's the motive? A simple robbery? There were hundreds of thousands of dollars of items the killer didn't take."

"That's the real puzzler, now, isn't it?" Connery sighed, as he gazed at the liquor bottle. He got up from his seat and opened the door. He called out, "We're ready to see the witness!"

*　　　　　*　　　　　*

Mrs. Mooney's mustard-colored shawl hung next to Martine's pea green waistcoat on a clothesline suspended over the potbellied stove in her kitchen. Small puddles of water gathered beneath the rain-soaked garments. The silver-haired flophouse owner poured cups of tea and honey. "I can't imagine what could be so important that ye stood in the drenchin' rain to wait fer me, Mr. Martin. Not that I mind, ye understand. I like a little company, but I hate to think that ye'll catch pneumonia because of me."

Martine sipped the steaming beverage. "This is good." He looked up and smiled. "I guess I needed some company, too, Mrs. Mooney. And I wasn't waiting very long."

The old woman pulled up a chair and sat across from her guest. "Well, I'm glad yer here. Tis seldom that I see any of my former lodgers on a friendly basis."

The tea warmed Martine's chest and stomach. He crossed his legs. It was the most relaxed he had felt in weeks. No ghouls lurking in dark corners. No demons prodding his legs from under the table. They feared Nora Mooney. Afraid of the childlike sparkle in her soft grey eyes; afraid of the dimples of innocence that still emerged through the wrinkles on her face; afraid of her plumpish arms that would offer hugs of comfort during times of fear or sorrow.

"Just from curiosity, is there a Mrs. Martin?" Nora Mooney asked.

"No, ma'am," Martine replied.

Nora sighed. "Such a fine gentleman, like you, not married? Ah well, tis different times. I was married when I was 15. George, the late Mr. Mooney, was 19."

"If it's not too personal, what became of Mr. Mooney?"

Nora looked sadly into her cup of tea. "Twas two years ago when Mr. Mooney was standin' on the corner of Chambers Street and Broadway picking up supplies. A team of horses broke loose from its carriage. Something scared them horses—what it was I never found out. Anyway, my poor husband was trampled badly. He died six days after." Nora made the sign of the cross.

Martine shook his head. "Horrible!"

Nora shrugged off her ancient grief. "Well, at least, he got to see his only child go to college. We had to wait twenty-two years before the Lord blessed our marriage with Patrick Aloysius. I was 37, and the doctors said it was a miracle that the boy and I survived!"

"Indeed a miracle, Mrs. Mooney," Martine replied. But Martine was quick to recognize the irony behind the blessing Mrs. Mooney had mentioned. The same forces that kept her barren for twenty-two years may have been responsible for spooking the team of horses that crushed her husband. And they may have been the same forces that sent the demons that tormented him.

Mrs. Mooney smiled. "I don't know why, Mr. Martin, but the Lord watches over me. He sent you here, in my time of need." She reached across the table and patted Martine's hand.

Instinctively, Martine retracted his hand from her warm touch. "I'm sorry," Martine said. "I'm not used to...contact."

"Why, yer just shy!" Nora said, smiling. "Ye have no need to be! A kind gentleman such as you!"

Slowly shaking his head, Martine replied, "That I'm not, Mrs. Mooney." He contritely folded his hands on his lap. "I'm a very bad man."

"Very bad men do not lend needy old women $40 without interest." Nora noted.

"It was stolen money," Martine admitted. He didn't think it strange that he would find a confessor in the silver-haired woman.

Mrs. Mooney sighed, "Who isn't a thief in these times, in this city? Yer only alternative is to starve."

"But you are not a thief," Martine stated.

"Aye. But like I said: the Good Lord watches over me."

*   *   *

Forty-seven year old Martha Adams, knots of grey speckling her kinky black hair, sat in a hot, ill-ventilated interrogation room. Opposite her were Superintendent Connery, Zachary Pembroke Farragut, and Inspector Robert Glavin. Martha nervously held onto a cup of water.

"Would ye like a shot of whiskey in that water?" Connery offered, with a wink. "I can fetch it."

Martha shook her head. "No, thank you, sir."

"Now, Martha, if I may call you Martha," Old Zack began, "you told two of Connery's men that you saw something unusual in the Hardwicke mansion at the time of the murder."

"The Devil," Martha whispered, barely audible. She did not look the men in their eyes.

Inspector Glavin scratched his yellow goatee. He was one of the rising stars of the force. Twenty-six years old, strong and handsome, he'd climbed through the ranks faster than any other officer ever. It was rumored, however, that he was ambitious, and desperately sought to become a Superintendent. "Would you please tell us, Miss Adams, how you know it was Satan?" he asked, doubtfully.

Martha shook her head. "Only the Devil would do what was done to the Master and the Lady."

"Did ye see him?" Connery asked.

"Yes, sir," Martha replied. "About three or four in the morning."

"And why were you awake at that hour?" Glavin asked.

"Who cares why she was awake?" Connery asked, somewhat irritated. "Let's just get a description."

Glavin, ignoring his superior, accused Martha, "You were drinking."

"Yes, sir," Martha admitted, ashamed.

Glavin shook his head. "This won't do. The woman was drunk, it was pitch black..."

Connery protested, "The woman is in the bloody house day and night! Drunk or not, dark or not, she can probably see things in that house in pitch blackness better than we could in broad daylight!" He turned to Martha, "Am I right?"

Martha, sensing Connery's support, looked up. "Yes, sir. That's true. And I only had one sip when..."

"When the Devil entered," Zachary said.

"Yes, sir," Martha replied.

Connery asked, "Can ye tell us, Martha, what he looked like?"

Martha nodded, "About my height."

"Five foot six, roughly?" Zack asked.

"Yes, sir," Martha answered. "White skin. Coal black hair, wild black eyes."

"You saw his eyes but he didn't see you!?" Glavin exclaimed. "Come now!"

Martha vigorously nodded her head. "It's true! He couldn't see me, sir. I was in the dark of the Ballroom. I was wearing a dark robe!"

"Go on, please," Old Zack requested.

"He come up from the cellar. I heared him."

Connery interrupted, "His footsteps?"

"No, sir. His voice."

"To whom was he speaking?" Old Zack asked.

"His followers!" Martha answered. "The other devils. He was saying things like 'Yes' then 'No' then 'I must get blood'. But there was no one with him that I could see. It must have been other devils!"

Glavin put his fists on his hips. "Ludicrous!"

"Quiet, Glavin!" Connery ordered. Then he asked, "What was his voice like? Describe it for us. Was it high-pitched?"

"No, sir. Low and hoarse-like. Like he didn't want to be heared by no one living."

"Did he have a weapon?" Zack asked.

Martha answered, "Yes, sir. A small knife. Maybe so big." She indicated with her hands that the blade was three-to-four inches long.

"The Devil didn't happen to tell you his name, did he?" Glavin asked sarcastically. "Or where he lives?"

"Glavin, blast ye…" Connery warned.

"He didn't have to tell me!" Martha shouted, surprised by her anger. "The Devil has a cloven hoof! And I saw the Devil, last night, dragging the burden of his cloven hoof!"

"He limped!?" Connery asked.

Martha nodded. "O, he did, sir! The Devil cannot walk the straight and narrow path because of his limp!"

"O, my God," Glavin muttered, realizing the implications of Martha's comment.

Old Zack turned to Glavin, then to an equally shocked Connery. "What is it, Mike?"

Connery looked to Glavin. "The Upstate Monster! The tramp!"

"It makes sense," Glavin replied. "Martine DelaCroix!" He was too shocked to be embarrassed of his previous skepticism of Martha's account.

"Who's Martine DelaCroix?" Old Zack asked, sweat dripping from the grey wisps of hair on his temples.

"Over the past few years, we've received telegraphs and wanted posters from several northern counties," Connery answered. "He's a burglar, and a killer. And they all mentioned a severe limp."

"And dark hair," Glavin added. "If I recall correctly, he'd been moving closer to New York City."

"He's a madman," Connery said. "Heaven help us!"

"Amen!" Martha said piously.

*   *   *

Just after dusk, Luigi heard the commotion. He rolled a display case before the front door. He put a dozen extra rounds of bullets in his vest pocket.

*   *   *

Ike Croft, just after dusk, heard the tumult. He lit his pipe, and sat by his window to watch.

*   *   *

Mrs. Mooney and Martine, just after dusk, heard the ruckus. "O, no!" Mrs. Mooney cried. "Bolt the door, Mr. Martin!" She ran for her shotgun.

*   *   *

The amber sun was setting, dragging the bruised, purple storm clouds with it. It had ceased raining, yet, the air was still thick with moisture. The sound of distant thunder was replaced by the incessant rumble of hobnail boots against cobblestones.

One wave of eight hundred Whyos, led by High Collar Browne, marched up Cross Street. Another wave of Bowery Boys, equal in number and then some, came up Orange. Long-legged Terry Billings led their procession. Judging by appearance, it was difficult to believe that the two groups were in alliance: The Bowery Boys wore tall dark hats; they sported walking sticks that doubled as clubs; and their tan great coats reached down to their knees. They all seemed fairly well-fed and clean-shaven.

The Whyos, on average were five-to-ten years younger than their allies, seemed hungrier and to have had limited access to shaving razors. Most of them wore short-brimmed caps and their tattered coats were of various lengths and colors. The only thing that made them look like brothers-in-arms was the genuine ice-cold hatred in their eyes for the enemy they were about to encounter. The war parties converged on the squat, three-storey former warehouse that housed The Dead Rabbits' main headquarters.

High Collar raised his pistol and fired a shot into the air. At the signal, scores of Whyos stormed the front door of the Rabbits' headquarters.

Brandishing axes, The Whyos broke down the door and raided the tenement. High Collar and Terry Billings stood smugly in the street, each envisioning Dead Rabbits being murdered while they ate their suppers. Anxious moments elapsed before members of The Bowery Boys and Whyos slowly emerged from The Rabbits' headquarters. Their daggers were bloodless. One member stood at the top of the stoop, scratching his head.

"Well, Geoff," High Collar called out, "did you get them?"

"Nay!" he responded. "There's no one about!"

"What!?" Terry Billings exclaimed.

"No one's home!" he called back. "There ain't a living soul or stick of furniture within!"

As if to support Geoff's report, a member of The Whyos poked his head out of a third floor window, and shouted, "The buggers are gone!"

"The hell we are!" Petey Daley shouted from the roof of The Rabbits' headquarters. "Get 'em, boys!" Dozens of Dead Rabbits tossed down heavy wooden chairs and tables onto the mob of Whyos and Bowery Boys. Across the street, from another rooftop, members of The Roach Guard, allied with The Rabbits, showered the rival gangs with buckets of broken bottles, sharpened bolts, rusted nails, and grappling hooks.

Terry Billings ordered his boys to retreat up the street, as did High Collar Browne. But with each building they passed, more heavy debris was dumped on them from adjoining rooftops: brickbats, slabs of stone, strings of chain, and chunks of cast iron fencework. At the ends of each street, large wooden crates and lit kerosene lanterns were thrown down, creating a wall of fire which trapped the unfortunate Bowery Boys and Whyos. The downpour of glass, steel, and stone was relentless. More lit kerosene lanterns were tossed into the middle of the throng. Dozens burned alive. Several more were temporarily blinded by the oily black smoke, rendering them helpless as more and more objects were hurled at them.

Petey Daley removed his pearl-handled pistol from his waistband. He aimed at High Collar Browne and missed. He aimed again. He missed again. "Bugger!" he shouted. "I need more fire-power. I need a rifle or a cannon!"

The second wave of Bowery Boys and Whyos tried to assist their comrades, but the wall of flame was impenetrable. Petey watched with satisfaction. He smiled, in spite of his inability to shoot down High Collar. His plan had worked.

A hare-lipped young man stepped over to Petey. He, too, smiled. His name was Max, and he was a former member of The Whyos. But he grew tired of High Collar Browne's ridicule about his disfigured mouth. He had no qualms about switching his allegiance to The Dead Rabbits. And he had been paid very well for his information. "I told ye they'd come at dusk."

"Aye, ye did, Max," Petey said. He shook the young man's hand. "Welcome to The Dead Rabbits!"

*   *   *

From the front window of the flophouse, safely a block away from the rioting, Martine and Mrs. Mooney watched Whyos and Bowery Boys flee. Martine noted the bloodied and burned young men, as they rushed by. Some were so badly wounded that Martine thought that his demons were blending into the mob. But they weren't. These were real people. Real blood. Real gore. In the near distance, the hellish flames continued to crackle through the twilight.

Nora cried. "Such a waste! Healthy young boys throwin' their lives away." She held her shotgun close to her chest.

"Why are they fighting?" Martine asked.

"Heaven knows!" Nora replied. "Anything sets these lads off! Tis rare if they didn't battle once a month! And the strange thing is that these boys—these gangs—were once a big help to the area. They used to assist people get to the polling places. Now they threaten people who don't vote for Tammany or the Know-Nothings. Once upon a time, they used to keep an eye out fer fires and help put them out. Now they start fires. I don't know what's happened to them: seems all they do is fight nowadays."

"They just fight?" Martine asked. "For no reason?"

"Look at this madness!" Nora said. Two members of The Whyos carried a fallen comrade between them; blood squirted from a gash on the boy's throat. "Can there be any reason in the world to cause all this?"

*   *   *

By the time Superintendent Connery, his men, and the fire brigade reached Orange and Cross Streets, The Whyos and Bowery Boys had already retreated into the night. Aside from the small stones that were hurled at them by children, the officers were immediately attacked by the stench of charred meat; nine Whyos and four Bowery Boys had burned to death. Other corpses—some crushed by stone and metal, others shredded to ribbons by the torrent of glass shards—littered the street and walkway.

Superintendent Connery held his handkerchief to his nose, as he stepped over the dead teenagers.

"Bloody Christ!" he muttered. He knocked on the battered front door of The Rabbits' headquarters.

"Come in, Superintendent," Petey answered from within.

When he entered, he saw several Dead Rabbits rearranging the furniture they'd stored in the cellar. Others laughed and drank freely from bottles of whiskey. A few slept on mats on the floor. Petey lounged on a sofa, a bottle of whiskey on his lap. "Good to see ye, Superintendent," he said.

"I'd say the same," Connery replied, "if the circumstances weren't what they are." He was irritated, not because the riot would create extra paperwork, but because it had interrupted his interrogation of Martha, which was left to Inspector Glavin and Zachary Farragut.

"Aye, tis a bloody shame what happened out there," Petey commented. He tossed an envelope to Connery, who, in turn, put it in his pocket. "Do ye need a hand cleanin' up that mess out there?"

"The day I need help from you and yer pigs is the day I better quit being a copper," Connery said.

"Pigs? Is that what ye called us?" Petey laughed.

Several of the boys grunted and oinked.

Connery looked around the room. "I don't have a much better word."

"And what makes ye so high and mighty?" Petey asked. He walked up to the Police Superintendent. "Ye don't like me much, do ye?"

"Am I supposed to?"

Petey put his forehead just under Connery's chin. "And why don't ye like me? We're both from County Kildare. Why, we'd be neighbors if we hadn't come here. Wouldn't ye like being my townsman?"

Connery stepped back but lowered his chin. "My townsfolk didn't murder and rob."

"Ah, no, of course not. And how much property did yer ma and da own before they came here? They didn't need to do much thievin' and murderin', did they?"

"Seven acres before the potato fields went bad," Connery answered. "And my ma and da didn't make it here. They died on the bloody boat. Cholera." Connery quickly scanned the room. He counted five objects he could quickly pick up and then slit Petey's throat with. "Don't speak ill of them!"

"Perish the thought, Mr. High-and-Mighty," Petey said with a smile. "The money they carried in their shoes is what got ye on the police force. Isn't it? But aside from that little wad of money, what makes ye different from me? What if ye came here without knowin' who yer ma and da were? Like me. Where would ye be, then?"

"I wouldn't be here," Connery announced.

"So says you. "

"Aye, so says me."

Petey wiped away the sweat on his upper lip. He laughed. He went back to his bottle of whiskey. "Well, then, DAMN ME! O, DAMN ME TO BURN IN HELL'S DEEPEST PIT OF SHITE! Har-har!" The alcohol on his lip mixed with the salty sweat. "I like ye, copper! Yer a tough bloke. If it weren't fer that little wad of money in yer da's sock...and that little envelope I gave ye just now...Yeeee! Yer a tough bloke. Very well, then. Very well. Boys, listen, Mr. High-and-Mighty has orders fer us, I suppose. Tell us, pigs, then, Sir Connery, what it is ye'd like us to do."

Connery felt the weight of the envelope in his pocket. Petey's reminder had stung him. He bared his teeth quickly.

Black Roger, who'd been standing behind Connery the whole time, put his hand on the Superintendent's shoulder. "Yes, what do ye want us do?"

Connery, unfazed, looked at Petey. "Fine, then! Help us remove them bodies. The quicker I'm out of this God-forsaken place the better."

"Aye," Petey responded. "Let's get ye out of here."

Connery headed for the exit. "And take that fancy gun from yer belt!"

"O, yes, sir! Your wish is my command." Petey laughed. He took the pearl-handled pistol from his waistband and tossed it on the couch.

          *   *   *

Martha was sent home at 9:30 by Inspector Glavin. When she got out of the pony and trap, Marian was waiting for her in the front hall. She had a snifter of brandy for Martha in her hand. When Martha entered, Marian noted the bruise on her temple. "Did they beat you bad?" she asked.

Martha shook her head. "No," she answered. She gulped down some brandy, "One policeman hit me, but the others was nice. They listened to me."

"They didn't whip you?"

"No."

"Do you have to go back there?"

Martha shrugged. "I don't know." She took another gulp of brandy. At first, the liqueur burned her throat, but it quickly eased its way down. "If I didn't like this here brandy so much, I never would have been through this." A yellow envelope on the chiffonier caught her eye. "What's that?"

"A letter," Marian replied. "For you."

"Kin you read it to me? I'm too nervous." Martha requested. She took another drink from the snifter.

Marian slipped a pair of spectacles onto her nose. She removed a piece of paper from the yellow envelope. "Let's see. Umm...says here:

Dear Martha,

How are you? I am fine. In fact, I am in love with a wonderful man—a silver merchant—from Boston."

"Boston?" Martha asked. "I thought she was in love with that fishin' boy from Canada."

"That was last week," Marian answered. She resumed reading:

I imagine that papa is furious with me. I don't care. As you once told me, you only get one chance to be young, so I am going to enjoy myself while I can.

I miss you very much. I hope papa isn't making you and Marian work too hard, and I hope he isn't driving poor mama mad. I will be home in a week. If I am lucky, I will bring home a husband—I so love Friedrich.

"Friedrich?" Martha exclaimed. "Lord."

Marian continued,

I think you will like my Friedrich very much. Would you bake your famous pecan pie for us? I can't wait to see you again. Please tell Marian that I said hello, and that I hope she is over her lumbago.

Love,

Joanna Rebecca

Marian replaced the letter into the envelope. "The po' child don't even know what happened yet."

Martha refilled her snifter. For the first time in over a decade, the dimly-lit mansion took on its haunted quality. Martha shivered, "I wish I didn't know what happened neither."

                    *   *   *

Amid the uneven clumps of earth that dotted the Potters Field on Hart's Island stood two small structures: the first, a latrine for the convicts who served hard labor—burying coffins, digging dirt, and so on—there during the day; the second, a small wood and tin shack that housed the caretaker, Hermann Graebel.

The wan, grey-haired man stretched his old bones across his cot. He kept a pot of coffee warming on a small, wood stove. A small, green jug of rum, well within Hermann's reach, rested on the floor.

He began reading about the murders of the Hardwickes, and the upcoming funeral, in *The Sun*. He scratched his eyebrow. "Heavens!" he exclaimed. "Three thousand dollars for each coffin!" He whistled. "I guess we're not all equal in the eyes of Mr. Death: the rich stay rich."

At ten o'clock, there was a pounding at the door of his shack. Hermann called out, "If you aren't dead, go away. This is a place for those who've passed on to get a well-deserved rest."

"Open up, ye old sot—it's Officer Cavanaugh," the good-natured voice replied.

"Officer Cavanaugh?" Hermann said, as he shuffled to the door. "It's a shame you've come here already. You're too young to be dead." He opened the door. "O! You aren't dead." He smiled.

The young officer smiled back. "How are ye, Hermann?"

"I'm fine," Hermann said. "But let us hope the time doesn't come soon when you arrive at this door and never leave."

Officer Cavanaugh laughed. "Yer in a morbid mood, tonight! Have ye been hittin' the bottle?"

"Yes, officer. And it hit back," Hermann replied. "Now, what can this old man do for you? Don't tell me another girl has poisoned herself at The Suicide Hall."

"Nay, it's worse," Cavanaugh said. He gestured to the horse-drawn cart that was parked by the field.

The old caretaker walked over and saw the score of bodies on it. "Another brouhaha in The Five Points?"

"Aye. Should keep the prisoners busy, eh?" Cavanaugh said. He added, "All these boys are unidentifiable. Even if they had families, they couldn't tell who is who. There were about 15 others whose families came and fetched them."

Hermann shooed away the swarms of flies that were feasting on the bodies. The burned and battered corpses lay on their backs, one atop another. "They're just children," Hermann sighed.

"Vicious children," Officer J.D. Cavanaugh commented. "Whyos and Bowery Boys, we're told."

The old caretaker shook his head. "Ach! And now, they are just dead children."

*　　　　　*　　　　　*

The dingy yellow nightshade flapped in the cool breeze. Martine, covered by a thin sheet, lay on his back in his bed. He had one arm draped over his forehead, the other straight at his side.

He slept a sound sleep. In a dream, he walked along a riverside in the sunshine. Trees bent in the wind. Tiny creatures danced about. Martine kept walking. No one impeded his way. No ghouls. No murder victims. No demons. Just sun and air and water and sky.

Even in dreams, the ghouls were stunned by Mrs. Mooney's effect on Martine.

*　　　　　*　　　　　*

"It could very well have been worse," Ike Croft told Luigi, as he examined the damage done to his haberdasher's shop: a crack in one of the windows and a singed awning. "Yes, it could have been worse."

"Those boys were pazzo—crazy, Signore Croft," Luigi said. "It looked like the end of the world. Everything from the sky fall down. Boom! It take me two hours to sweep the walk."

"You did a good job, son," Ike noted. He handed Luigi a dollar bill. "You kept the shop safe, and you cleaned up. I'll bet you'll be glad to get home after a night like last night."

Luigi shrugged, "I don't know."

"What? Family troubles?" Ike asked.

"Little bit," Luigi admitted. "My Maria, she's going to have a baby."

"Congratulations, old boy! Maybe now you'll get that daughter you've always wanted."

"Maybe," Luigi said. He shook his head. "But, Signore Croft, it's different. When Maria was having the boys, she was happy girl. Now, she cry. All the time cry. Her mama no talk to me—she never like Luigi, now she hate Luigi."

Ike hoped he hadn't flinched. He wondered if it was his child that Maria was carrying. He remembered how he had lied to Maria and claimed to have the power to deport her mother, if Maria didn't give in to his sexual demands. He remembered telling her, "If you don't come back to my flat, I'll have The Dead Rabbits come here and murder your sons. And if you're thinking of telling your husband, I'll personally murder your whole family." He remembered the sneers from Maria's mother. He could still see the tears in Maria's eyes whenever he undressed her, the way she bit her lower lip when he pinched her nipples, the way she closed her eyes and softly wept when he pushed his way into her warmth.

"I don't know, Signore Croft," Luigi finally sighed. "Maybe you right. Maybe it's a girl, and that's why she act crazy now."

"Yes, son," Ike said smiling. "I'm sure that's what it's all about. Now, go on home. Here, take this extra dollar for doin' such a good job. Go and buy the wife a nice present."

Luigi refused the dollar. "No, Signore Croft. I'm sorry. I no should bother you with my—how you say?—problems. God bless

you, Signore. Arriverderci." For the first time that Ike could
remember, his young employee lost his strut. Stoop-shouldered
and head down, Luigi left the haberdasher's shop, and headed
home.

Ike exhaled, in relief.

     *   *   *

Although the funeral for the Hardwickes had been delayed
three days, so that Miss Joanna Rebecca could return from Boston
and attend, the story had not vanished from the press nor from the
conversations of many New Yorkers. So when the day of the
funeral finally arrived, most of New York's celebrities, politicians,
and dignitaries, including Mayor Fernando Wood, District
Attorney Zachary Farragut, Superintendent Connery, and
Inspector Glavin, attended the services at Grace Church.
Hundreds more stood outside in the light drizzle, and thousands
of others lined Broadway, so they could, once the ceremony
ended, catch a glimpse of the hearses, as they made their way
down to the Hamilton Ferry. The ferry would then transport the
funeral party to Brooklyn, where Cornelius Augustus and Agatha
Jane Hardwicke would be laid to rest in Greenwood Cemetery.

In the front row of pews in the spacious splendor of Grace
Church, a plump Joanna Rebecca Hardwicke sat between Martha
Adams and Mayor Wood. Joanna's uncle and aunt, the Masters,
sat with unshakable restraint directly behind her. Joanna wore a
traditional black mourning dress. An impenetrable veil covered
her face. When she lifted it to wipe tears away, the curious
stretched their necks to get a view of her: it had been rumored that
the young woman was not particularly attractive—only her
money was. Those who saw her thin lips, smallish grey eyes, and
broad, turned up nose had their suspicions confirmed.

At the altar before her were the silver coffins containing her parents' bodies. The minister solemnly blessed each coffin, and went through with the ceremony. On occasion, Martha patted Joanna's hand to comfort her. It was unusual for a black woman to occupy such a prestigious seat for a public function, but Joanna had demanded it.

Joanna, during the voyage home, had admitted to herself that the death of her father was secondary to the loss of her beloved mother. Mother had understood Joanna; Mother had defended Joanna; Mother had loved Joanna. Now kind-hearted Martha was the only person in the Hardwicke Mansion that Joanna could say she really loved.

She watched the reflection of rows upon rows of yellow candles glimmer on the coffins. The heat was stifling, especially under the veil. She felt she was unable to breathe. Slowly, almost gracefully, she slid off her seat and collapsed on the floor.

Pandemonium erupted. Superintendent Connery raced to the front of the church. Martha slapped the young woman on the cheeks, "You're okay, Miss Joanna. You're just a little faint. Take off this here veil."

The crowd anxiously watched the young lady stir. Sitting undignified on the polished wooden floor of the church, Joanna slowly came to. Martha, being the closest to her, became clear in the girl's vision. She threw her arms around the tough, tired maid's neck. She sobbed convulsively, "O, Martha! What shall I do, Martha? Look at what has been done to Mother and Father! O Martha!"

Martha held the girl close to her cheek, and caressed her hair. "Shh, now, Miss Joanna, shh. Everything will be just fine." Had Joanna seen the tears in Martha's eyes, it would be doubtful that she'd have been consoled.

"Is there anything I can do?" Superintendent Connery offered.

Joanna continued crying.

"Aww, now, shh, " Martha hushed. She wiped Joanna's tears away with a handkerchief. Turning to Superintendent Connery, Martha said, "Mr. Connery, sir, I know you are a good man; you treated me nice. So take no offense, sir, but I think the young miss, here, would be more at ease, if this Devil that done what he done to her folks was caught. A little justice goes a long way to helpin' somebody get over her grief." She held the young woman closer. "Shh, now, Miss Joanna. Easy now, easy."

All eyes turned to the Superintendent.

*   *   *

When Luigi arose to go to work, he found his wife napping beside him in their bed. Not wanting to disturb her, he grabbed his shoes and tiptoed over her and the other members of the family who slept on beaten mattresses at the far end of the bedroom. A shiver ran through him when he entered the kitchen, and saw his mother-in-law waiting for him at the dinner table. A bowl of beans and pasta steamed at the center of the small table. "Sit down," she said sternly in Italian.

Luigi sat, "Is this for me?" he asked.

"No, it's for the Pope! Now eat," she ordered. "And listen to me."

*   *   *

Ike Croft paced impatiently and nervously in his haberdasher's shop. Martine was too dangerous to keep around. The funeral of the Hardwickes had amplified the public's outcry for justice. Ike could clearly be prosecuted as an accessory-after-the-fact in the murders. The implications were too staggering: Ike could, at the very least, spend the rest of his life on Bedloe's Island. No matter how profitable he was, Martine had to go.

Martine stepped into the haberdasher's shop, just before closing time. "Hello, Ike," he said. "Would you like to get some supper?"

"How are you, Martine?" Ike said. He forced a smile. "Supper? Hmm...No, I don't believe I should. Feel a bit of a cold coming on."

"Nothing serious, I hope."

Ike shook his head. "No, I doubt it." Then he added, "You know, maybe it's a good idea if you didn't eat out in public, as well. You can't count on your good luck too long: someone could recognize you."

Martine replied, "There aren't any coppers in this neighborhood. And they don't have a very good description. Did you see the drawing they had of me in *Leslie's Illustrated?*"

Martine was feeling invincible. His daily visits to Nora Mooney kept the demons away, somehow. At times they visited him in dreams but not as prevalently as they'd used to. He'd had one recurring dream: he and Mrs. Mooney would stroll through the bucolic environs of upstate New York. Mrs. Mooney would comment on the golden sunlight that combed through the leaves of treetops on nearby hills. Martine would point out to her the scenes of the abominable crimes he'd committed. The victims would still be lying there, bloodied and putrefied. Their eyes would open; they would rise. If Martine became afraid, Nora would make the sign of the cross. "Do not torment this man!" she ordered. And the ghouls would obey and lie back down. "Rest in peace," Nora would tell them. The corpses would reply, "Thank you, ma'am." Then they'd close their eyes, and smile. And Martine, in his sleep, also smiled.

In his waking hours, Martine was also at peace. As he'd stated, the descriptions of him in the press were mostly inaccurate: some still described him as having a beard. He knew that as long as he remained in The Five Points, he'd never be found, especially if

Superintendent Connery remained in Petey Daley's pocket, and if Ike Croft remained friendly with Petey.

Even Ike was aware that Martine was fairly safe in The Five Points: Ike knew that Martine had introduced himself to everyone else as "Martin"; and that the artists' renditions of Martine were no less than awful. Yet, someone, someday would put it all together—the dark eyes, the severe limp, the name Martin—and cash in on the hefty $1,000 reward Joanna Rebecca Hardwicke was offering. "Yes, Martine, that drawing was terrible. You are charmed."

Martine smiled, "I guess." He looked around. "Where's Luigi?"

"It's what I wonder!" Ike exclaimed. But Ike was hardly thinking about his night watchman. Martine's presence enervated Ike. He wanted Martine out. "Here, son, do me a favor, will you? Run down to the boy on the corner and get me an evening edition of *The Post*."

Martine shrugged, "Of course."

While Ike prayed that Martine would get trampled by a horse and carriage—or, at least, that Luigi would finally arrive— Martine casually walked up the street. But a dark thought crossed his mind: Ike Croft never read the evening papers, as far as Martine knew. And Martine never saw Luigi bring one to him nor did he remember Ike picking one up whenever they walked home together. "And why did Ike seem so preoccupied just now? Am I walking into a trap? Or an ambush?" he wondered. "Did he send Luigi to fetch the coppers? Is that why Luigi is not in the shop?"

At the corner, a young boy of about eight years hawked his newspapers. Nobody on the street seemed suspicious: shopkeepers, dockworkers, and the such, hurried home before the twilight turned to night. Martine approached the boy.

"Paper, sir?" he asked.

"Yes," Martine searched for a penny. "*Post.*"

"Kill him!" the boy ordered. Blood and brain tissue oozed from an axe wound on his forehead. "Ike Croft is going to have you arrested! Kill him!"

Martine blinked.

The boy, fair-haired and light-skinned, studied Martine's frightened expression. He asked, "Sir, are ye feeling ill?"

"O," Martine said. "Yes, a little. Here." He gave the boy a penny.

"Thank you, sir," the boy replied.

Martine tucked the newspaper under his arm, and turned toward the haberdasher's shop. A child's voice behind him instructed, "Give me Ike Croft's blood. Kill him!"

Martine dropped the newspaper and ran. When he got to Ike's shop, he saw blood dripping down the inside of the glass. "They are in there!" Martine gasped. "O God, they are in there!" He would not enter the shop and witness what the ghouls had done to Old Ike. He ran to Mrs. Mooney's flophouse: he decided he would spend the night there. He had to.

∗   ∗   ∗

MISS JOANNA REBECCA HARDWICKE COLLAPSES AT PARENTS' FUNERAL; HER MAID BLAMES POLICE SUPERINTENDENT CONNERY FOR THE FAILURE TO CAPTURE SUSPECT MARTINE DELACROIX

announced the next day's headline of *The New York Times.*

CANADIAN MURDERER STILL AT LARGE
The Sun printed in two-inch high letters.

But perhaps the headline that galled Superintendent Connery the most was on the front page of *The World*:

WHY CAN'T THE POLICE FIND THE HARDWICKES' KILLER?

Agitated by the press statements, Connery could not eat his early lunch. He tossed the newspapers aside and stewed at his desk. The large banner above him read, "Faithful Unto Death". It had depictions of street scenes in which policemen performed various duties: rescuing an elderly woman from a fire; rustling up stray carriage horses; assisting lost children, etc. He wished it also depicted the capture of Martine DelaCroix.

Inspector Glavin entered the office, unannounced as usual. He bore a grin that stretched from ear to ear. "Good morning, Superintendent."

"What are ye smilin' about?" Connery asked.

"I've given this crime a great deal of thought and I think I've solved our problem in finding Martine DelaCroix," Glavin announced.

Connery despised the smug look on Glavin's handsome face. "And what might that be?"

"We've been looking for him in the wrong places," he answered.

Connery rubbed his hangover. "Obviously, else we would have found him."

Glavin pulled up a hardback chair and sat. "We have been concentrating our search too much on the vicinity of the murder scene. However, we know that DelaCroix is Canadian and has roamed around upstate. He can't adjust to city life so quickly. I'd wager that he's either up in Westchester or The Bronx." He folded his arms, confidently.

Connery responded, "Listen, lad, it is standard police procedure to investigate and concentrate our search in the vicinity of a crime scene. The criminal might return, after all. And, if DelaCroix is upstate or in The Bronx, I'm not goin' up there!" But Glavin's notion made Connery think, "Or the bastard went the other way! Downtown, to The Five Points! Anyone can disappear there!" But something else led him to believe that The Five Points held the key, but could not remember what it was. He looked at Glavin, "Hang on," he said. "Maybe ye have a point there."

"I think I do," Glavin said. "How many men can you give me?"

"How many do ye need?" Connery asked.

Glavin's bloated ego prevented him from being suspicious of Connery's unusual acceptance of one of his speculations. "Ten, at least."

"Ten it is, then!" the Superintendent said. "Go up there. Maybe something will turn up. Or someone'll talk. And to go along with your reasoning, let's not forget Staten Island as a possibility."

Glavin's grin grew wider, if that were possible. He rose from his seat. "Thank you, sir! With any luck, we will catch the monster."

"I hope ye do, son," Connery said, as he watched the proud young man walk out of his office. "Ye dopey son of a bitch," he muttered. He reached into a drawer and pulled out a bottle of whiskey, and drank. Then, he ate his breakfast biscuits. Suddenly, he exclaimed, "Ah, bugger! Now, I know what it was!" He ordered his secretary to have a pony and trap waiting for him out front.

*　　　　　*　　　　　*

When the mail arrived, Mrs. Mooney stopped sweeping the stoop, and sorted through the envelopes. On one, she recognized her son's handwriting. She put down her broom, put on her spectacles, and sat on a step. Normally she would wait until night to read Patrick's letters, but she wanted to know if he received the money she'd sent him. Anyway, it was a brilliant, warm morning, so she treated herself to this little break from her daily chores. She gently ripped open the envelope, and read:

Dearest Mum,

I thank you, and may The Good Lord bless you, for the money. But I must ask, who is this Mr. Martin? Can you trust him? Perhaps he is one of those confidence men about which you so often hear. You know the old ruse: he'll lend you money without interest and then you pay him back. Since you've established trust in each other, he will ask you for a similar loan; you will give it to him, and then he vanishes forever. Please be careful.

However, if he is simply a kind soul, then give him my heartfelt thanks, as my schooling has benefited from his generosity. Now, I can confidently state that my grades will be better than they ever have been.

These warm spring evenings remind me that I shall soon be home. I cannot wait for the day when I see you again.

Love,

Patrick Aloysius

"Ah, the dear lad," Nora Mooney said. "If ye only knew how proud I am of ye." She kissed the signature on the page, and folded it back into the envelope.

Martine opened the front door of the flophouse and startled the old woman out of her deep admiration for her only child. "Good morning, Mrs. Mooney," Martine said.

Mrs. Mooney looked up, shading her eyes from the sun with her hand. She could see that the rims of his eyelids were blood red. "Morning, Mr. Martin. Why, yer a sight! Didn't ye sleep well?"

"Ah, no. I have a lot on my mind," Martine replied. In fact, he had not slept at all. Every time he dozed off, he envisioned Ike

Croft being brutally murdered in a variety of ways: shooting, clubbing, knifing. Had he killed Ike and didn't know it? Were the ghouls now independent of Martine and killing without his knowledge? And what worried Martine the most was the fact that his demons had returned while he slept under the same roof as Mrs. Mooney.

"I'm sorry to hear that, Mr. Martin." Nora said. "Perhaps I can ease yer mind a bit." She showed Martine the envelope. "My son has received the money, and he thanks ye—as do I—fer the assistance you've given him. God bless ye, sir!"

The news did cheer Martine a bit. "I'm glad to be of help."

"Say," Mrs. Mooney interjected, "aren't ye late fer yer job?"

"I'm not working today," Martine replied. "I was wondering, however, if I might ask a favor of you."

"Name it," Mrs. Mooney said.

"As you know, I was locked out of my apartment last night," Martine lied. "I was thinking, would it be possible for me to stay on here, and deduct the rent from the money I lent to you?"

Old Nora remembered her son's warning about confidence men. She remembered that Martine confessed to being a bad man, and that the money he had lent her was stolen. Still, he looked like such a sad, tired little man, who sincerely relished her company—almost like a child who returns to his mother after a long, frightening separation. "T'would be a pleasure, Mr. Martin," she smiled.

The two shook hands on the deal.

*   *   *

Superintendent Connery knocked on the new front door of The Dead Rabbits' headquarters. The hare-lipped young man, Max, answered.

"I'd like to see Petey Daley," Connery said.

The boy noted the brass badge on the Superintendent's uniform. "Hang on, I'll get him."

"Max! Let my friend, the Superintendent, enter!" Petey called from within. Young Max held the door open for Connery. He was very impressed that Petey Daley had a friend in the Superintendent.

As Connery stepped through the building, he acknowledged, with a tip of his cap, several of The Rabbits who played cards or unpacked cartons of stolen goods. He noted, however, an unusually immense wooden crate, at least twelve feet long and five feet tall, on which was stenciled, "Property of the U.S. Army". He asked, "What's in the crate, Petey?"

The leader of The Dead Rabbits caressed the wooden box. "Just a little insurance package, Mr. High-and-Mighty. Ye can't be too careful in this wicked old neighborhood." He smiled, "Now what is it ye want?"

Connery replied, "I was wonderin' if ye would oblige me with a favor."

"Well, well," Petey smirked, "since when can us pigs be of use to ye?" He took a gulp from a bottle of premium whiskey and offered it to Connery.

"I suppose I shouldn't believe that I'm as high-and-mighty as I've been acting, lad." He accepted the bottle and took a hefty swig. "Good whiskey, son. Delicious." He wiped his mustache. "Look. I know ye owe me nothin' outside of our arrangement with Tammany. But what I have to ask of ye concerns us both. This is of mutual interest, if ye understand me. Will ye help?"

Petey nodded. "Go on."

"The other day, when we were cleanin' up the streets of corpses, ye had a little gun in yer trousers."

"Aye, this one," Petey removed the pearl-handled pistol from his back pocket. "Tis a beauty, eh?"

Connery nodded. He held out his hand. "That it is. May I see it?"

Upon hearing this, several Dead Rabbits, like vultures over an animal carcass, closed in on Superintendent Connery.

Petey held up his hand. "Tis fine. Relax, boys. I think it's time we start trustin' the Superintendent." He handed over the weapon. "Careful—it's loaded."

Without having to hold it up to the light, the Superintendent could see the ornate carving on the inlaid pearl. He could also read the initials *CAH*. "Let me ask ye, did ye ever wonder about these letters on the handle?"

Petey shook his head, "Nay. I can barely write me own name. I assumed it was the name of the gun's maker. What's it say?"

Connery replied, "Tisn't the manufacturer's name, Petey. What it says is that ye can go to Bedloe's Island fer a long time, if ye don't tell me where ye obtained this weapon."

"It can say, 'I'm going straight to hell,' Superintendent, but I won't tell. I never peach on a fellow."

"I'm not talking about peaching," Connery informed Petey. "Tis a matter of saving yer hide."

"How so?"

Connery held the gun out, "It says there, 'C-A-H'. Do ye have any idea what that stands fer, lad?"

Irritated that Connery, for the second time, was forcing him to acknowledge his illiteracy, Petey frowned, and shook his head.

"Cornelius Augustus Hardwicke," Superintendent Connery said.

Stepping back from the pistol, Petey said, "I didn't do it, Superintendent! I don't go into people's homes and..."

Connery interrupted, "I know ye didn't do it, lad. It's not yer style."

Petey wiped away the beads of sweat that began to assemble at the edge of his upper lip. "Aye. Tisn't me style."

"So, where did ye get the gun?"

The Dead Rabbits' leader shook his head.

"Petey, son," Connery began, "this is not a business arrangement or personal disagreement between you and me. This is bigger than both of us. The Mayor, the Governor, people from Tammany...they want this man, and they'll do anything to get him. They'll destroy me; they'll destroy District Attorney Farragut; they'll send down the state militia to destroy you and yer gang, if they thought that ye was concealing information. Now, I promise ye, I'll not implicate you or yer men in any investigation. Just tell me where ye obtained the weapon, and that'll be the end of it."

"Go on, tell him," the huge Black Roger advised. "This is serious. I'm just the hired muscle around here, Petey, but I don't think this would be considered peachin'!"

"I'd tell him," square-jawed Jimmy Slocum said. "We don't need no militia comin' down here. And, Jayz, the Hardwicke weapon!"

Several of Petey's men nodded in assent.

Petey Daley, who'd never peach on a friend, looked to the floor. He sighed, "A fence: Ike Croft. Runs a haberdasher's up Orange." Then Petey looked up, "But Superintendent, it wouldn't be his style either to murder a family in their beds. He's an old man."

"Someone in his ring, then?"

Petey rubbed his chin. "Hungry Frank? No. Kid Gas? No. Ho! Wait!"

"What is it?"

"He's got a new man. Queer fellow. Ah, what is it? Matthew?"

Connery felt his heart beat faster. "Martine?"

Snapping his fingers, Petey exclaimed, "Aye. That's got it! Martin! Man about me height. Had a bad leg. I remember that now."

"A limp?" Connery asked, running his finger along his lower lip.

"Bad one!" Petey said. "'Tis about all I can remember. Have I helped?"

What he was about to say made Superintendent Connery smile. "Lad, ye might have helped yerself to a $1,000 reward."

Petey tilted his head. "Well, isn't that bloody nice?"

∗   ∗   ∗

After erecting a light-weight wood frame he'd just purchased, Martine began unpacking his large leather suitcase in his private corner of the flop area. He felt he had made one of the better decisions of his life: moving into Mrs. Mooney's flophouse would do wonders for him. He already felt better: "No demons here."

"Mr. Martin?" Nora Mooney called out.

"Yes?"

Mrs. Mooney stepped behind the screen, and inspected it. "Very nice!"

Martine smiled. "Thank you."

The plump old woman put her hands in the pockets of her apron. "I have some tea brewing in the kitchen, and some chicken and biscuits on the stove. Would ye care to join me fer a little dinner?"

Martine bowed, "It would be a pleasure, Mrs. Mooney."

Pleasure? No, that was not the word Martine really wanted to use to express his feelings. *Blessing* was probably more precise. As Martine eagerly followed the kind-hearted woman across the flop area and into the cluttered little kitchen, all he could think was,

"I'm safe. I'm happy. This is good. I don't deserve so much happiness."

        *   *   *

The lightly breaded piece of halibut sizzled in the frying pan. Two sections of lemon, each about the size of a silver dollar, were dropped upon it. Purple slices of Bermuda onion were then tossed into a bowl of boiled green beans.

Martha got hungry, as she cooked lunch for Joanna Rebecca Hardwicke. She helped herself to a piece of pumpernickel bread, and spread a dollop of sweet butter on it.

Old Marian returned to the kitchen. She had an empty crystal fruit cup in her hand. "I think Miss Joanna is getting her appetite back."

With her mouth full, Martha said, "Thank the Lord. I was getting worried."

"You always took care of the girl, Martha. You don't have to worry so much now. The worst is done with." Dunking the cup into a wooden tub that was filled with soapy water, Old Marian added, "She'll be fine."

Martha helped herself to another dollop of butter, and said, "I don't know about that. I seen what I seen, you seen it, Miss Joanna seen what she seen…No. Who's to say that any of us will be fine after that?"

        *   *   *

The front door to Ike Croft's haberdasher's shop was unlocked. Superintendent Connery slowly turned the white porcelain knob, and entered. He kept his other hand on the pearl-handled pistol.

The splattered blood on the front window, dark brown and dried, told him that violence had taken place in there within the last 12 hours, perhaps 18. Rats scattered along the wooden floor.

Connery grabbed his handkerchief and held it to his nose. The smell of corruption was nearly overwhelming. He listened to where the sound of buzzing flies was most prevalent. Near the front of the shop, behind a cracked glass display case, he found the body of a middle-aged, heavy set man. Connery correctly assumed that it was Ike Croft.

The victim had been shot once through the head. Connery could tell that Old Ike had had his back to the front window when the bullet entered his face, just under the right eye. The exit wound at the back of Ike's head was massive: otherwise it would have been impossible for so much blood and brain matter to have been sprayed onto the glass. Closely inspecting the window, he saw the inch-wide hole where the bullet had penetrated, after it had left Ike's head.

Connery turned back to the corpse. He saw that Ike's throat had been slashed open by what was probably a straight-edged razor, as well. The Superintendent shook his head, "The monster did this to make sure the poor bastard could not live to see today. How did he know I was onto him?"

*   *   *

Spending their lunch breaks together, Hermann Graebel and Officer J.D. Cavanaugh sat on wooden crates outside the caretaker's shack in Potter's Field. They ate the old caretaker's special chicken stew from tin plates. Cavanaugh noted, "I see ye got all them Whyos buried quick."

Hermann nodded his head. "Had to. The sun was strong yesterday. And those dead children were already exposed to the elements too long."

The young wavy-haired officer dunked a piece of bread into his stew, and then stuffed it into his mouth. "And if those convicts had been in the sun too long burying them…"

"Then other convicts would have had to bury *them*!"

Cavanaugh scanned the barren landscape. No trees, no flowers, no shrubs, not even grass: no sooner would a seedling take root, when it would be unearthed to bury another "person unknown". Cavanaugh belched as he continued staring at the rows upon rows of dark brown rectangles of earth. "I'll say this: it's an awful cheerless place here to spend one's final rest."

Hermann shrugged his bony shoulders. "It's not so bad."

The young officer raised his fork to emphasize what he was going to say. "Greenwood! Greenwood Cemetery in Brooklyn: where they buried them Hardwickes. Now that's the place to enjoy eternity! Out there in the trees and the hedges, the air is so clean. Would make ye feel important to be buried there with the famous folk."

"Greenwood!?" the old caretaker exclaimed. He spat out a sliver of chicken bone. "That's no place to get rest. It's a park, not a cemetery, with all those fancy play areas and park benches!" He lifted the rim of his plate to his lips and slurped some gravy. "How could you possibly get any rest there with all those screaming children running all over your grave? Ach! That isn't rest; that isn't peace. That's Hell!"

Cavanaugh shrugged.

Hermann continued, "Now, here, this place," he spread his arms, as if unveiling a magnificent vista, "this is where you'll find eternal tranquility. Nobody comes here: no children, no blubbering mourners...Sometimes another guest is laid to rest near you, but you know he'll be quiet."

*   *   *

Mrs. Mooney and Martine finished up their lunch. Martine removed the cloth napkin from his collar. "That was a fine meal, Mrs. Mooney. Delicious."

The old woman lifted the dishes off the table. "I always say the simplest meals are the best."

"That they are," Martine concurred. "Here, let me help you." He rose from his chair and grabbed the sponge by the washtub.

"O, no," Mrs. Mooney protested. "No guest of mine does dishes. I'll hear none of it." Just then, however, there was a knock on the front door. "Heavens! A boarder this early in the day?"

"Now, I'll have to clean the dishes while you tend to your customer," Martine said smiling. He took the dishes from her hands. "Go ahead, and answer it."

Mrs. Mooney wiped her hands on her blue-and-white-checked apron, and plodded to the door.

Martine dipped the sponge into the washtub. He made quick spiraling motions with suds along the stoneware surface. The food felt good in his stomach.

"Yes, officer?" he heard Mrs. Mooney ask.

Martine dropped the dish into the water.

"Good afternoon, ma'am," Superintendent Connery said, tipping his tall cap. "Are ye the owner of this rooming house?"

"I am," Mrs. Mooney replied.

Martine quietly stepped out of the kitchen and sneaked into Mrs. Mooney's office. He could see and hear Mrs. Mooney and Superintendent Connery talk.

"Ma'am, do ye know an Ike Croft, a haberdasher up the street?" Connery asked.

Old Nora nodded, "Aye, but not on a personal level, mind ye."

Something scratched at the back of Martine's neck.

Connery announced, "I regret to inform ye that Mr. Croft has been murdered."

Martine turned around. A skeletal figure appeared in the periphery of his vision, and then vanished. Without realizing it, he had picked up Mrs. Mooney's double-barreled shotgun. Both chambers were loaded.

Mrs. Mooney brushed back a wayward lock of her white hair. "O, dear, not another! This neighborhood has gone to Hell in a hand basket! Was it from the rioting?"

"Nay," Superintendent Connery answered. "'twas much later than that. At least, a day later. I've been checking the local boarding houses, because landlords, like yerself, see so many people come and go. Perhaps ye might have run across a stranger, new in town, who might have been acting suspiciously."

Martine raised the shotgun and aimed it through the slight opening of the door. The back of Mrs. Mooney's head, round and silver-haired, was in his sight. "Kill her!" he heard someone say: it was the woman from Dobbs Ferry. Not quite 30, not quite beautiful, and not quite dead, in spite of the fact that her forehead ended abruptly above her right eye and her cranium was empty. She sat tensely behind Mrs. Mooney's desk. The bodies of her two sons lay in a bloody, lifeless embrace beneath it. "You killed me; now, kill her. I want to taste her blood, just like you tasted ours. Kill her!"

"No!" Martine whispered.

Nora was going to mention Martine to the Superintendent, solely because he was a stranger, and had admitted to being a bad man. But a murderer!? She could not believe that. "No, sir. No one very suspicious. And certainly not one who'd murder anyone. But I see all kinds of people."

Sweat broke out on Martine's brow. He whispered to the ghoul, "How did you kill Mr. Croft? I don't recall doing it!"

"What *do* you recall?" the ghoul asked back. She leapt from the wooden chair and pointed at her sons. "You remember coming into my home and murdering me and my children, don't you!?"

"Forgive me, forgive me, forgive me..." Martine whispered. He kept his aim on the back of Mrs. Mooney's skull.

Superintendent Connery, standing in the strong sun, removed his cap. "Well, we are searching for one particular suspect."

Martine could see where the buckshot would tear into Nora's head: just above and behind her right ear.

Connery asked, "Have ye, in the last few days or weeks taken in a strange boarder? The person we are looking for is not from this area—actually he is a Canadian. He has a bad leg, and may go by the name of Martin."

That was enough for Nora to hear. Martin may have been a good man and good company, and he may have helped her son with his education, but he was wanted by a lawman now. As much as it distressed her, she was going to tell the policeman that, yes, she did know a Mr. Martin who has a limp, and that he was just inside the next room. But the awful, ear-shattering shotgun blast prevented her from saying anything at all.

*   *   *

Sitting on the steps of The Dead Rabbits headquarters, hare-lipped Max looked toward the flophouse up the street. "Did ye hear that?"

Petey Daley, spit-shining a grapefruit-sized cannon ball on his lap, said, "Aye."

"Well, shouldn't we go see what it was?"

Disinterestedly, Petey replied, "It was just a gunshot."

"Oh," Max said.

"There! Ain't she a beauty?" Admiring his handiwork, Petey held up the sparkling projectile: a black sun against a bright blue sky.

"Aye. That she is!" Max said with a smile.

*   *   *

Kid Gas and Hungry Frank heard the gunshot from Abie's restaurant around the corner. With his mouth full, Hungry Frank asked, "Think The Whyos are at it again?"

"No," Kid Gas replied. "They aren't that foolish." He rubbed the eczema on his forearm against the edge of the table. "They took enough of a beating the other day, I would think."

*   *   *

Superintendent Connery drew the pearl-handled pistol, and pushed Nora Mooney to the floor, "Stay down!" he ordered. The air in the tiny foyer was heavy with the smell of gun powder.

"My God, what's happened?" Nora asked.

"Just stay down!" Connery shouted.

The door to Mrs. Mooney's office was slightly ajar. Grey gun smoke trailed from out of the opening. Connery cocked back the hammer of the pistol. "Martine DelaCroix! Come on out! This is the police!" With more than a decade of police experience under his belt, Connery knew he must remain calm. But this was Martine DelaCroix, the upstate monster, strangler, slasher, bone breaker, the most wanted man in six New York State counties. Connery had trouble keeping the gun in his hand steady, but he did. "Martine DelaCroix, this is your last chance! Come out or I'll fire. I swear I will!"

Connery heard no response, except for a steady dripping sound. He grabbed the glass doorknob and entered the office, pistol first.

In the center of the floor, Connery discovered the body of a remarkably small, yet muscular, man. A smoking shotgun lay diagonally across its torso. Where the head should've been was an indistinguishable mass of bone, blood, and brain tissue. More blood, which had been sprayed up to the ceiling, dripped onto the Superintendent's shoulder.

"Holy Jay-zus!" Connery muttered.

"What's happened?" Nora called out, still cowering on the floor of the foyer.

"Don't come in!" Connery advised. "Ye have a holy mess in here. He's blown his head clean off, sweet Christ! Please, just stay where ye are. Ye don't want to see this!"

"O, Lord, no," Nora cried. Summoning as much strength as her old bones could provide, she crawled out of her prone position and knelt down to pray.

It would be up to one's beliefs to decide whether the demons continued their torture of Martine in some blazing cavern of Hell or they were finally dissipated with the scattered buckshot, allowing Martine to find tranquility. However, Connery could not explain away the tremendous feeling of relief, of a calm of immense magnitude, that had settled upon the room; not because the city and world were now rid of Martine DelaCroix, the Upstate Monster, but because whatever fear or torment, hate or anguish, that compelled this tramp to put the barrel of a shotgun under his chin and end his life, was also gone. Because Connery quickly perceived that this monster was not a monster. He thought, "If he had been, why didn't he kill Mrs. Mooney or me? He had all the time in the world—and a powerful weapon. But this man did not want to kill anymore."

Although far from being a religious man, Superintendent Connery made the sign of the cross with the hand that still held the pistol.

*   *   *

The next morning, Joanna Rebecca Hardwicke and Martha rode in a polished brougham to Greenwood Cemetery. Joanna held onto a bouquet of white lilies to rest on the grave. The brougham rattled along the cobblestones of Flatbush. Above the farmlands of Brooklyn, where hunters sought out rabbit, thin streaks of white clouds made their progress across a blue sky.

"It's a nice morning," Martha noted.

"Yes," Joanna replied. As she observed the herds of goats and cows, the flocks of chickens, and the farmers that tended to their crops, Joanna wondered if there was another wandering madman making his way through the back roads of these isolated regions. Then she made a mental note to write out a check to one Peter Fergus Daley, for his help in bringing her parents' killer to justice.

*   *   *

In the gold and crimson lighting of St. Mary's Church, in the rearmost pew, Nora Mooney wept silently. She grieved for the poor little soul who'd committed self-slaughter in her flophouse. "Whatever evils he committed, Lord, forgive him. He was not a wicked man. He was more like a penitent soul. I believe that he was like the Romans who tortured and murdered yer only Son— he did not know what he was doin'. Or why.

"Wicked men do not lend desperate old women $40, do they? And they don't keep lonely old ladies company, when their sons are 50 miles away at school, do they? Do wicked men make tired old ladies feel happy again? Or make them feel needed again?

Because, in some way, I know he needed me." She rested her forehead against her clasped hands. "But, Lord, do ye think *he* knew how much he meant to *me*? O, I do hope so, Lord, with all my heart!"

* * *

The sunlight streamed through the windows of Superintendent Connery's office. He was about to sip his morning tea, when he picked up the newspaper. He put down the porcelain cup and roared, "WHAT!" The editorial in *The World* read:

...and in his handling of the Martine DelaCroix case, Superintendent Michael Connery has demonstrated profound ineptitude, once again. There are several reasons for this thesis, but let us look closely at the two that are most prominent.

First, when he sought Martine DelaCroix, the Superintendent lacked the requisite intuition to investigate the Sixth Ward, known to be this city's breeding ground and sanctuary for criminals. Instead, he sent ten of his men and his Chief Inspector to The Bronx. While his men fruitlessly searched those remote nether regions only days after the tragic, senseless deaths of the Hardwickes, Martine DelaCroix was enjoying the life of a murderous thief in The Sixth Ward. For sport, Mr. DelaCroix shot to death an innocent haberdasher, Mr. Ike Croft. There is little reason to doubt that he intended to do harm to his landlady, a widow, Mrs. Nora Mooney.

Perhaps what must gall every decent citizen of this metropolis is Superintendent Connery's failure to capture, bring to trial, and convict Martine DelaCroix. Having ascertained the monster's hideout, Superintendent Connery did not call for assistance. Thereby, he endangered the welfare of the elderly Mrs. Mooney. Superintendent Connery afforded DelaCroix enough time to search for Mrs. Mooney's weapon and commit suicide: to end his life by his own choice which was a luxury he did not extend to his victims...

Superintendent Connery couldn't read any further. "Bloody Know-Nothings." He crumpled the newspaper and hurled it in the direction of the wastepaper basket. His anger made him thirsty. He put on his cap and decided he would spend the rest of the day drinking at The Suicide Hall.

*   *   *

At the head of his new, long dining room table, in his new, larger apartment, Luigi said grace over the stuffed capon, bowls of pasta, and kettles of steamed mussels. He stood up and clasped his hands, while the rest of his family bowed their heads in reverence. In a Sicilian dialect, he softly said, "Thank you, Lord, for safely bringing us to America—the only place where we can feast on your beautiful foods. Bless my family, who works very hard. Bless my wife for all she has done and all she has suffered. Bless her mother for showing me the path that a true man must walk to defend his family's honor. In the name of the Father, and of the Son, and of the Holy Ghost..."

The entire family joined in with an "Amen".

"Let's eat!" Maria's mother shouted.

Of all the members of the family, Maria ate the hardiest. The combination of her horrific experiences with Ike Croft and her steady diet of cheap, and often unsanitary, foods had caused her daily nausea. Her pregnancy scare had been just that. And although it was close to three weeks late, her menstrual cycle resumed, also affected by the bad food and stress. "It's good to not eat like a dog," she commented.

"For once," Luigi's mother-in-law began, "we can even say, 'God bless Mr. Croft.' The pig." She spat on the floor. "May the Devil torment him for a hundred thousand years."

"He will," Luigi said, as he helped himself to a dishful of mussels. "He will because after I sent him to his grave with that," he pointed to the short-barreled rifle that leaned on a far wall, "I made sure he couldn't plead his case before Saint Peter with this." He held up the sharpened carving knife that rested next to the capon. "He will have a hard time speaking to anyone with his throat cut out."

"Too bad you didn't take all his money, Luigi," his mother-in-law said. "But the seven thousand dollars you took is more than enough to keep us fed and warm. And to bring the rest of our family over here." She rose from her seat, and walked over to her son-in-law. She grabbed Luigi by his cheeks and kissed him several times on his forehead. "You saved this family from disgrace, Luigi. We are all very proud of you. May the good Lord protect you and all of us." She kissed him once more.

END OF THE FIRST BOOK

BOOK TWO

WONDERFUL BASTARDS
(1860)

Rudy and Ted spotted the mongrel as it sniffed at a heap of refuse. It was not an unpleasant looking dog: a brown and white mixed breed, shaggy and small, but not as emaciated as most of the strays that wandered the streets of Lower Manhattan. Its fur, however, was matted and filthy, splattered by coaches and carts wheeled through the piles of slush, mud and horse manure that punctuated the grime of Chatham Street.

The two men stopped to examine the dog from a distance. Rudy removed his stovepipe hat and scratched the scalp beneath his red hair. "What do you think? A Brumaire?"

Ted nodded. "I believe it may be."

Rudy, sometimes called Rudy Red, removed a small tin container from the pocket of his tattered, blue great coat. He took off the lid and pulled out a chunk of near-rancid pork. He knelt down some ten feet away from the dog and whistled while waving the meat. "Here, love. Here! Here!" Rudy had learned that when approaching these strays you had to keep your distance and offer a bribe. You just couldn't walk up to one and whisk it away. You simply had to earn its trust and let it follow you.

The dog pricked up its ears and, cautiously, trotted over to Rudy. It stopped a foot or so away and sniffed the meat.

"That's right, love, all for you," Rudy said smiling.

Ted pulled out a leash from inside his coat.

The dog gently bit into the morsel and began chewing. Rudy reached out and scratched behind the dog's ear. "Yes. Good fella. Yer a good fella, ain't ye? Yer not like those bad dogs raised in the gutters. Yer lost, ain't ye? Ye got some meat on ye, don't ye? Somebody took care of ye." When the dog finished eating, it wagged its tail and licked Rudy's fingers. "Such a friendly little thing! Ye want more, don't ye? Well, ye just come with us, boy. We'll give ye more, 'cause yer a fine dog!"

"Come, now! Are ye done talking to the animal, yet? Or should I get a bloody priest over here to marry ye?"

Rudy continued talking to the dog. "O, don't pay nasty Teddy any mind. He's mad at the world. He comes here to escape the famine in Ireland—next thing ye know he has to go fight the bad ol' Confederacy. When he comes back here, his wife is gone, no jobs...Now, he wasn't as smart as I was, ye see. I joined the Volunteer Services, instead of becoming a Billy Yank."

Ted threw the leash at Rudy's feet. "Just put that on the bastard and we'll be off. It's too bloody cold."

Rudy inspected the black leather leash. "This is nice. Where'd it come from?"

Ted wiped his dripping red nose. "Traded fer it at Callahan's. If we're going to call this thing a 'Brumaire', it ought to have a fancy expensive leash. Am I right?"

"Of course, sir," Rudy laughed. "Yer always right." He bent over and whispered into the dog's velvet ear, "Actually, Teddy's the dopiest bastard you and I will ever meet."

"Yer in a mood today," Ted noted. "Took a nip of drink?"

"Guilty, sir. Just a nip." After adjusting the clasp on the leash, Rudy stood up. "All right, love. Let's go home."

The two men and their newly-acquired companion walked toward Orange Street and their rooming house. Shards of glass crunched along with the pebbles of ice under their hobnail boots. "Looks like The Plug Uglies were bored last night," Ted inferred, as he pointed to the smashed gas lamps.

"Or The Dead Rabbits," Rudy added.

On the steps of their tenement, a teenage boy had just finished injecting himself with the morphine he'd stolen from nearby Bellevue Hospital. He looked up at the pair of bearded men and their dog. "Hey, grifts. What's this? Is this yer new sweetheart ye got on the leash?" The dog, sensing that the boy was paying attention to it, trotted to him and nuzzled its head between his knees. The boy obliged and began petting it. "Are ye their girlfriend?"

Ted grabbed the leash from Rudy's hand and jerked the dog back. He said to the boy, "Why aren't ye down at the docks peddling yer sister's arse, Nosey?"

"To hell with YOU!" the boy shouted. "I had some news from The Uglies but to hell with you! I'd just as soon as…"

Rudy flipped a nickel onto the boy's lap. "Now, there, Nosey, take care. Teddy, here, is in a foul temper 'cause of the bad weather. Pay him no mind. What's the news?"

Nosey Cunningham, whose nickname derived from his large, bulbous nose, still had his lip curled at Ted. He spat onto the slush on the pavement. Then he looked into Rudy's deep green eyes. "I'll tell *you*, Rudy. I got no use fer that sot ye keep company with. Why is he yer partner? I'm not a bad one. I can work with ye. You always been good to me Rudy. A fellow can always look at ye and say, 'There goes a nice man.' Do ye know that's what I think whenever I see ye? I says, 'Rudy Red, he's a fine fellow.' *But him*...When I see that ugly black-bearded bastard..."

Rudy tossed another nickel onto Nosey's lap. "The word, Nosey! What news have ye? 'fore ye pass out."

Nosey clumsily deposited the coins into his shoe. He bent forward and patted the dog's head. "I know what you are planning to do with the dog."

Ted shouted, "Well, if I ain't beholding the wisdom of Solomon himself! Everybody in the bloody neighborhood knows what..."

Nosey nearly fell over as he tried to get to his feet. "Well, don't ye be doing it anywhere south of Fourth Street anymore! Another couple of grifts tried it on Bleecker and almost got killed there. A lot of folks are wise to it now." Nosey dropped back down onto the steps, the numbing effect of the morphine beginning to take its solid hold. "To hell with you."

Rudy lightly slapped Nosey on the cheek. "Thank ye, son."

Nosey shrugged. "To hell..." He embraced his knees. "Damned cold."

Rudy nodded to Ted. "Get his legs."

"Let the bastard freeze," Ted growled.

"Now, Teddy, ye know we can't do that."

"Why not? The reformers want to clean up the neighborhood. We'd be giving them one hell of a head-start."

"It just isn't right," Rudy said. "And since when are you on the side of reform?"

Ted grabbed Nosey's ankles while Rudy reached under the boy's armpits. Nosey resisted mildly, but was too far along the path to oblivion. The pair lifted him up and carried him into the less frigid hallway of the boarding house. The two men and their dog began climbing the stairs. Suddenly, Ted stopped and turned back down. He walked over to Nosey and removed the semi-conscious boy's shoe. He took out the two nickels and mumbled, "To hell with *you*, bastard."

In a few hours, the dog was bathed and the men had changed into their newly-stolen outfits: Rudy into a well-to-do businessman's suit, complete with pocket watch, and Ted into a conservative waistcoat and hat. As they walked up Broadway, they discovered a new saloon on 17th Street. Rudy grabbed the leash and stepped in.

"Afternoon, sir," the bartender said.

The establishment, for the most part, was empty since it was well after lunchtime. The bar was close to thirty feet long. Its carving depicted lascivious little cherubs prancing about a life-size rendition of a naked and permanently bored Aphrodite reclining on a seashell. The brass foot rail and spittoons were meticulously polished. Behind the liquor shelves were three immense mirrors. Above the central mirror, a wood-carved American eagle seemed to burst forth from the wall.

"What'll you have, sir?" the bartender asked.

"A beer," Rudy said. "And may I help myself?" He gestured to the dozen hard-boiled eggs that rested in a green glass bowl.

"Certainly, sir. We aren't Delmonico's but we try our best."

As Rudy ate, he checked his appearance in the mirrors. Rudy was 32 years old but the red beard, streaked with some gray, lent him the appearance of being five to ten years older. However, if you looked closely into his eyes, which were forest green and free of wrinkles and lines, he actually looked much younger than his years. "Devilishly handsome, ain't ye?" he whispered to his reflection.

"Here's your beer, sir," the bartender announced.

Rudy sized him up: "Not even old enough to grow a proper mustache. Hair the way they still wear it in Ireland. The boy just got off the bloody boat." He asked, "Can you make change of a ten, son?"

"I believe I can," the bartender said. When he returned with the change, he said to Rudy, "Queer dog. I haven't seen one like it."

"It's a Brumaire. French Canadian," Rudy said proudly. "They can cost $75."

"Tis an awful large sum to pay for something that will die on ye some day."

Rudy laughed. "True. But I only paid $20. A competitor of mine lost thousands in the market in '57. Thousands. I offered him twenty for the dog, and he took it. He's a fine dog!"

For a quarter of an hour, the two chatted on the variety of topics that crammed the day's headlines. Rudy then consulted his pocket watch. "Lord! Is that the time?" he exclaimed. He pulled five dollars out of his pocket and put it on the bar. "Can you help me, son? I have a very important meeting in five minutes that I cannot miss. Would you keep an eye on the dog until I get back? I'll just tie the leash to the foot rail. He won't be a bother and I promise to return in less than a half an hour. Please."

The young man eyed the money.

"You'd be doing me a great favor," Rudy added.

"Certainly, sir," the bartender said. "Mind ye, I leave in an hour."

Rudy Red tipped his stovepipe hat. "Bless you, son. I'll be back presently!" he turned and hurried across the sawdust-covered floor to the exit.

For a few minutes, the bartender wiped beer steins and shot glasses. After the dog got over his initial despair at being left alone, it sniffed curiously at the foot rail and floor. Occasionally, it sneezed whenever it got a snootful of sawdust. "Bless ye," the bartender said each time.

The door swung open. Black-bearded Ted strolled in and removed his hat. "Good afternoon," he said to the bartender.

The dog wagged his tail and yipped.

"Hello, little one." Ted said with a smile.

"What can I get for you, sir?" the bartender asked.

"Brandy, please. Mind ye, none of the watered-down stuff ye usually get in the places around here."

"I can assure ye that we don't serve anything like that in this fine establishment, sir."

"Glad to hear it," Ted said with a smile.

The dog yipped louder and more furiously.

"What's the matter?" Ted asked the dog. He knelt down and stroked the dog's head. "Say, this is a Brumaire, isn't it?"

"That it is," the bartender said, bringing over a snifter of brandy.

"Is it yours?" Ted asked, placing a few coins on the bar.

"No, sir," the bartender replied.

Ted laughed. "I'm relieved. The day a bartender can afford a Brumaire is the day I realize I'm in the wrong business." Ted sipped his brandy.

"A gentleman was in here just before you walked in, and left it while he attended a meeting." With a mild dig, he added, "It seems that he found this place trustworthy enough. And he gave me five dollars just to watch it."

"I would dare say," Ted remarked. "It's a valuable dog. Worth about fifty dollars, I guess."

"Seventy-five dollars," the young man said.

Ted continued stroking the dog's head.

"Let me ask you," Ted began, "when is this gentleman due to return?"

"In 20 minutes or so."

"Twenty minutes, eh?" Ted took another sip of his brandy, and then placed ten dollars on the bar. "Look, I apologize fer what I might have said about this fine establishment or about yer trustworthiness. I'm just in a foul temper. But how's this, then? I give you ten dollars and you give me the dog. You tell the gentleman that the dog scampered off. None will be the wiser."

The bartender shook his head. "I'm sorry, sir. I can't do that."

Ted dug deeper into his pocket and put an additional two dollars and change on the bar. "Here! That's all I've got. What say ye?"

The young man continued shaking his head. "Sir, please, I can't do it."

Ted deliberately thickened his Irish accent. "O, come, now. I can tell yer from home. Killarney, I'd say. We both can make some money from this. Ye can't possibly earn much as a bartender, and I can certainly use some money."

The young man became adamant. "Yes, I'm from Killarney. But I still can't sell ye the dog. There is the reputation of this establishment at stake, and beside, I like the gentleman and I would like *him* to return as a regular client."

Ted took the money from the bar, except for a few two-cent pieces. "Can't find fault with a man for trying, can ye?" After finishing off his brandy, Ted wiped his lips, and smiled. "Good day to ye, lad." He adjusted his hat, buttoned his collar, and exited in no particular hurry.

The dog jumped and barked in outrage and fear.

"Quiet!" the bartender shouted.

Suddenly, Rudy ran into the bar. His hair was in disarray and his face was beet red. "Ruined! I'm ruined! Lord, what am I to do?"

The bartender put down his bar mop. "What is it, sir? What's your trouble?" He could see the tears in Rudy's eyes.

"Swindled! I've been swindled!" Rudy cried.

"Calm yourself," the bartender said, sympathetically. "Can I get you a whiskey?"

"A whiskey? A whiskey? And what good would that do? My bloody business partner took every penny I have! O, Lord!"

The bartender poured the whiskey anyway. "Here, sir, drink this. It'll calm you down."

Rudy greedily drank the whiskey. "The bastard," he hissed. "I'll murder him."

The bartender's mouth fell open. "Sir! Please, don't speak of murder. Be reasonable. Have you notified the authorities?"

Rudy nodded. "Yes."

"Well, I'm sure they'll catch the thief."

Rudy stared into his empty glass. "What good will come of it? The bastard will have it spent before he's caught."

The bartender refilled the shot glass. "You mustn't think that way. The Lord will see to it." He then offered a comforting smile.

Rudy looked at the bartender and gave a small smile back. "Maybe he can get back my pocket watch, as well." Rudy indicated with his thumb that his vest pocket was empty. "I had to pawn it, in order to make rent." His smile soon faded, however. The tears welled up again. "Ruined. I shall be living in the streets before too long. If I could only get a hold of a few hundred dollars, I could go down to Wall Street and make a good investment. That would give me a start. But...Who am I deceiving? I'm finished. As good as dead, I am."

The bartender gave Rudy a sympathetic pat on his hand. "Now, sir, I'm awful sorry for your loss. But do take heart. I wish there was something I could do for ye."

Rudy nodded. "So, do I."

The dog resumed its whimpering, confused by Rudy's avoidance.

The bartender looked at the dog. He smiled. "Ye know, sir, I have an idea that can benefit both of us." He dug into a blue jar behind the beer mugs. "I don't have a few hundred dollars but I do have some money. Been hiding it from me wife." He counted through the bills. "Thirty-seven dollars. Now, you take this money, and you give me the dog."

"What!?" Rudy shouted. "These dogs cost $75. I couldn't sell it so cheap!"

The young man gave Rudy a dark, reproachful look. "Now, sir, you yourself admitted that you acquired this dog under similar circumstances. Am I right? You paid only $20 to a man who was in your unfortunate situation."

Rudy looked as if he were embarrassed. He nodded, then sighed loudly. "This is true, son. Perhaps it's some kind of justice." He looked into the boy's eyes. "Very well. I'll take the money. But on one condition."

The young man put the money onto the bar. "What's that, sir?"

"The condition is," Rudy stated, "that you NOT sell the dog for two weeks. By then I shall have made some money, could afford to repay you and then some, and take my dog back."

The bartender extended his hand and shook with Rudy. "Done! Now, if this isn't a deal among gentlemen, I don't what is."

Rudy took the money from the bar and put it in his pocket. "Bless you, son. Now, just so you know, the dog is to be fed twice a day. Nothing too fancy, mind you. Scraps of meat, pork, and the such. Once a week, put a raw egg in his food. It's good for his coat."

The young man nodded. "I'll do that."

Rudy extended his hand. "God be with you, son. You are doing a good deed for a fellow human being. You are saving me and I can never repay you enough for that. I shall see you in a fortnight." Rudy tipped his hat, smiled, and hurried toward the door.

"Sir! Are ye leaving so soon?" the young man asked. "Please, rest yerself. Have a drink with me, on the house!"

"The market closes in less than forty-five minutes," Rudy replied. "And it's always business before pleasure, son. However, do keep a pint of beer cold for me, and we shall drink together in two weeks."

"One thing more, sir, before ye go!"

Rudy hesitated.

The young man asked, "What's the dog's name?"

Rudy turned, and, grinning, replied, "Teddy!"

Rudy left the establishment and stepped into the cool drizzle. Walking across Broadway, he found Ted beneath the statue of George Washington at the southeast corner of Union Square Park, their prearranged meeting spot. Ted was twirling his hat on his finger. By the smile on Rudy's face, Ted could tell the plan was a success. "Well, sir, how have we done?"

Rudy Red nodded. "We have done just fine, my friend. Thirty-seven dollars. Well, minus the seven dollar investment."

Ted pursed his lips.

Rudy nudged his friend. "Ye look thirsty. Let's get us a steak and a lot of ale. We quite earned it, I dare say."

"I agree," Ted said.

     *   *   *

District Attorney Zachary Pembroke Farragut unbuttoned his black frock coat as he entered Gosling's Restaurant. He removed his silk hat and brushed back the few wisps of hair behind his ears. After twice scanning the enormous eatery, which served over a thousand customers a day, he spotted Police Superintendent Connery, who was sitting at a small table in a corner of the room. Zachary smiled and gave an acknowledging nod, as he headed toward his friend. To Old Zack, Michael appeared anxious: his foot tapped nervously under the table and his fingers drummed along its top. However, Old Zack could see a smile beneath his friend's thick black mustache.

"Zack! I'm glad ye could make it!" Michael said.

Zachary took a seat opposite his friend. "There's always room in my book for you, Mike. This old bachelor doesn't have many engagements after working hours."

"Nonetheless, I appreciate it," Michael said with his toothy grin spreading further. "Especially since I hardly gave ye any warning. Now what'll ye have?"

"O!" Zachary exclaimed, seeing the waiter who'd popped up behind him. "A pint of ale and bitters, please."

"And whiskey for me," Michael ordered. "Fact, make it a double."

"A double whiskey?" Old Zack asked. "What's happened? Another riot in The Sixth Ward?"

"Nay," Michael replied. "But I think one is coming—tis in the wind. Probably between them Bowery Boys and The Dead Rabbits." Connery shrugged dismissively. "Nothing's to be done about it. So long as The Rabbits stuff the ballot boxes fer Tammany Hall and I pay Tammany fer me job and The Rabbits take care of me—all is as it should be, I guess."

Zachary sighed, "As long as the money goes around and around."

And once again Old Zack felt sympathy for his friend's unenviable position. He could not fathom what it was like to be a Superintendent of Police who was fired by an indefatigable goodness and yet was continually besieged by corruption and malice. The corruption was unavoidable: it touched every citizen—especially public figures—like the heavy soot in the air. If you were impoverished, you were lured into taking money in any way you could. If you were well-off, there were ways to get richer. And if you were somewhere in between and were not tainted by avarice, like the Superintendent of Police was not tainted, there were ways of being intimidated into taking the graft. The malice from the citizenry that Connery was sworn to protect was equally ubiquitous. Much of this enmity was fueled by the Nativist, Know-Nothing press which continually hounded the Irish-Catholic Superintendent, as it did anyone who was not of a White Anglo-Saxon Protestant heritage, and especially now that Civil War was over and they could focus their spleen on him.

Zachary imagined that in another time and, especially, in another place, Michael Connery would be the exemplary Superintendent of Police. Zack had no such fancy about any of the other Police Superintendents or Commissioners he'd known over the years.

Connery smiled as the waiter placed the drinks on the table. "Ah, thank ye, son!" he exclaimed. "Now then, give us two steaks, well done, with all the trimmings."

Old Zack raised a bushy white eyebrow. "Steak? I fear I haven't brought enough money for a steak dinner, Mike."

"I'm buying." Michael announced.

"O, no, no, I won't hear of…"

"Please, Zack, tis the least I can do fer me best man!"

Zack's other eyebrow went up. His thin lips spread into a smile. "Best man?"

Michael nodded. "Correct, friend. I'm going to be wed!"

"Well, now, if that isn't wonderful news, I don't know what is! And it's well about time, I'll add. Who's the lucky lady?"

"One Elizabeth Shaw, a beautiful redhead from County Meath," Michael answered, with a hint of pride. "Arrested for soliciting, charges dropped. Asked to be my bride, offer accepted!"

"Well, well, I remember the girl. No wonder you were so keen on having my office drop the charges. That and the fact that there was no proof of her guilt." Old Zack said, raising his glass, "Well,

I'm glad you're finally going to do it. Here's to you, Michael. Congratulations. I wish you many years of happiness." The two men clinked glasses and drank.

Michael wiped his lips with the back of his hand. "So, will ye do it—be me best man?"

"How could I decline?" Zack responded. "I'd be honored!"

"Very well then!" The two men drank again. When he put down his tumbler, Michael noticed that the waiter was still standing by the table. "Lad, what is it?"

"The steaks, sir. You want two?"

Michael laughed. "There are two of us here, aren't there? What's the problem?"

The waiter nodded. "Well, sir, I heard the gentleman accept your offer to be your best man—and congratulations, sir—but I did not hear him accept the steak."

*   *   *

Fifteen year-old Katie Cunningham sat on the edge of the bed, in her assigned room in The Suicide Hall saloon and brothel. She counted the coins her pimp and owner of the establishment, Cyril Stephens, had given her. One dollar and twenty-five cents. She pondered over Cyril's generosity; she would have had to have been with five men, normally, to make such money. That day, however, she had only been with four. This made her uncomfortable: the other girls had once warned her about Cyril's generosity.

It didn't matter though.

Frank would return in two days. And then this would be all over. No more filthy men pawing at her, drooling on her, hurting her inside. No more brother to keep an eye on and feed. Nosey was becoming too much for her to handle. As her older brother, he should have been raising her, not the other way around. But ever since they had run away from the orphanage, two years earlier, she had to tend to her morphine-addicted sibling—the sibling who had sold her Cyril.

But no more. Enough was enough for Katie.

Frank was nice. He was only eighteen. The other men on his whaling ship had teased him into coming to the whorehouse. But when he saw Katie, tiny, little girl, blue-eyed Katie, and when Katie spoke with him, they fell in love with the speed and sureness as only the young can.

She looked out the window. There were a lot of men coming in from the docks. It would be a busy night for the other girls. Not for Katie. Katie was finished for the day.

She removed her bedclothes and put on her stockings and dress. She wrapped her long raven-colored hair into a braid and pinned it at the top of her head. Then there were four knocks on the door. Cyril's signal.

"I'm done for today," she called out.

Cyril opened the door. He was a stout man who wore the same brown, plaid suit day after day. He always appeared to be in the grip of a fit: eyes bulging, bright red skin, quivering jowls. "Katie, my dear, I need your assistance."

"But I'm just getting ready to leave," she stated.

Cyril nodded. "I know, I know. But I'm a businessman who must satisfy his clients, love. My friend, here" Cyril reached out the door and pulled in a leering middle-aged man with missing front teeth, "my friend here, John, he likes his girls young and beautiful. And, face it, Katie, you're the prettiest youngest girl I have."

As if to agree with Cyril's evaluation of Katie, the customer's grin grew wider, a string of saliva bridging his lips.

Katie looked down. "I thank ye kindly for the compliment, but I must be off."

The customer slowly walked over to Katie.

"Now, Katie," Cyril said, "my friend has already paid for your service. Now, be a love, and do me this one last favor for today."

Now Katie knew what the extra coin was for. She could detect the sour smell of liquor on the man's breath, as he pet her hair.

"She's very pretty," he said, "and sweet." He reached down and cupped his dirty hand on her breast.

"Hey," she said, pushing the man's hand away. "I didn't say I would do it." She turned to Cyril and said, "I'll give you your twenty-five cents back!"

"I don't need it," Cyril said.

The customer reached down and stoked Katie's pelvis.

"Stop, I said!" Katie cried, giving the man a shove.

The man stepped forward and punched Katie in the ribs. "Lie down, wench!" he yelled.

Doubled over, Katie tried to run away, but the customer grabbed her. He slapped her face. The front of her dress came apart in his fist.

Cyril turned toward the door. Before stepping out, he said, "Thank you, love. I do appreciate the favor." He closed the door behind him.

"Frank will be here in two days," Katie recited over and over in her head, while the man threw himself on her, pushed her legs apart, and entered. "Frank will be here in two days."

*   *   *

A heavy, wind-swept snow fell suddenly upon the city at dusk. Thick, heavy flakes swarmed around the gas lamps like hordes of moths in the summer. The hack Rudy and Ted had hired rolled silently down Third Avenue, as the feathers of snow muffled the usual clatter of wood and iron wheels on uneven streets.

Rudy spied a little girl that was standing at the gutter; she was begging for alms. The girl, dressed in nothing more than blue rags, shuffled her bare feet. Her blood smeared the gray curbside ice.

"Child!" Rudy cried out, as he pulled a couple of two-cent pieces from his pocket. "Here!" He tried to toss the coins into the girl's cigar box but missed.

The girl hurried to retrieve the money. She looked up and watched the black carriage with its two golden headlamps flicker between the snowflakes. She smiled. "Bless ye, sir! Merry Christmas!"

Even through the snow, Rudy could see the large red blotches on her cheeks and forehead: smallpox. She had been scarred for life. "Bless yerself, child!" Through his inebriation he remembered all too well his days as boy, fighting with fist and foot for a street corner where he could peddle newspapers. When, at sixteen, his dashing good looks emerged, he charmed his way onto those corners, and then into people's confidence. For over a decade, he worked the grifts: grifts for tourists, grifts for gamblers, grifts for the religious, etc. For extra money, he worked in brothels, posing as the husband of the prostitute the client was in bed with, demanding payment before calling for the police. But when he met Ted, the ugly, battle-scarred, Ted, he realized he had met his match. Ted could not be fooled. Ted was too smart.

"Bless yerself," Rudy Red yelled again, although the girl was already out of earshot.

"Keep givin' money to every wretched child in town, and we'll need ten thousand Brumaires," Ted muttered into his gnarled black beard. He would have growled those words but the full meal and pints of ale placated his disposition somewhat.

"We need a new idea," Rudy said. "We can't bloody well sell a dog to every saloon-keeper in New York."

"Aye," Ted muttered. He sat back, pushed his hat over his eyes, and folded his arms. "I'll think of something."

Rudy picked his teeth with a matchstick. This was what vaguely frightened Rudy about his association—albeit a profitable association—with Ted. Ted was the brains and the brawn. He was as cutthroat with his mind as he was with tongue and fists. He was bigger and stronger than Rudy, and faster and more fierce with his fists. True, Rudy was the better actor, the handsome charmer, the one who gained the confidence of everyone he targeted.

But Ted, he knew it all. His life in the streets of Antebellum New York, and his camaraderie with the pickpockets, grifters, and fences, some from Philadelphia, some from Boston, who happened to find themselves fighting The South, gave him the added edge to become the premiere trickster of Manhattan. He knew how to find out which warehouses would be left unattended, or which guards could be easily plied with alcohol. He knew how to identify the types of men who would forget how much money they had left on the bar or would be tempted to gain someone else's money while actually losing their own.

But, most importantly to surviving in The Five Points, Ted knew how to stay on the good side of all the Irish gangs while remaining anonymous to the other groups. The Whyos, The Roach Guard, and The Dead Rabbits all liked Ted. True, Ted did cut them in on every substantial theft he'd pulled off, but they genuinely liked him. Perhaps it was his independence that they admired—they'd all tried to recruit him but to no avail. Or maybe it was his ability to pull off whatever grift he'd set his mind to. Whatever it was, Ted was clearly a respected man in The Sixth Ward. But where it came to a grift where he needed some finesse, some charm, and a lot of good looks, he had neither the talent nor resources. When he met Rudy, he knew he had someone with which he could create an unstoppable partnership.

"Yer still the dopiest bastard I ever met," Rudy mumbled.

"Aye, fer working with a fool like you," Ted replied with a grin.

The two men rode in silence for the duration of the ride. Once they got to the outskirts of the neighborhood—since they knew that no carriage driver in his right mind would go into it—they paid the driver and left a generous tip. The driver thanked them and hurried the hack through the snow.

Along Mulberry Bend, they encountered Petey Daley, leader of The Dead Rabbits. "What say ye, Teddy? Evening, Rudy Red."

"Looks like we may have ourselves a big snow, tonight," Rudy observed.

"Aye," Petey said. "It usually keeps the neighborhood quiet." With a smirk, he added, "But when the snow stops, people need coal and food badly. And these *people* will do anything to get it. Understand me?"

Ted gave Petey a wink. "Aye."

"I don't think we were planning to go out tomorrow, were we Teddy?" Rudy asked.

"I think not."

Petey gave Ted a soft punch on the biceps. "Very smart. Take good care." Petey put his hands in his pockets, his fingers around a revolver, and went his way.

The wind grew stronger in force, rushing the snow almost parallel to the ground. The cobblestones and the frozen ooze became increasingly slippery.

"What people do ye think it was Petey spoke of?" Rudy asked. "The True Blues?"

Ted shook his head. "Last week, Petey and a few of his Rabbits 'borrowed' eight bins of coal and a few racks of beef from The Bowery Boys' stock house. So when The Boys go looking for it all tomorrow, and find their stock house raided, they'll go looking to see which gangs aren't out looking for food and coal. They'll find

The Uglies and The Whyos out there looking, since those men had their stock houses confiscated by the coppers. But they won't see Petey or his Rabbits out there looking. And The Boys will put it all together."

"The Rabbits are calling for a war then?"

Ted shrugged. "Why not? Petey could afford it. The Uglies just had a todo with The Whyos, and a lot of those lads are in jail or the hospitals. The Daybreak Boys have all but disappeared into the air. So if The Bowery Boys want to go against The Dead Rabbits one against one, well, it don't look good for The Boys."

Rudy laughed. "How do ye know these things?"

"Well, instead of beginning my mornings with a nip of liquor, I walk around the neighborhood and listen to people. I get information," Ted replied. He saw that Rudy was put off, as usual. "Aye, but don't fear. These are my concerns. Your concern is to execute whatever plan I concoct. You are better at it than I. I can dream up some scheme but you have the gumption and talent to do it. No easy task, my friend."

Rudy's belly was too filled with food, and his eyelids too heavy with a desire to sleep, to continue the discussion. Anyway, Ted had acknowledged that Rudy was valuable and talented, and that Ted needed him. Something Ted rarely admitted.

When they arrived at their boarding house, Nosey Cunningham was still in the hallway. He sat up against the wall and picked the lice from his trousers. "Hey, grifts."

"How are ye, Nosey?" Rudy asked.

"Odd," Nosey answered, scratching his scalp. "Did I see you two this afternoon? With a dog?"

"No, ye did not," Ted snapped.

Nosey shook his head. "Then I had to have dreamed it. Ye had a dog with ye, to pull off the trick. Then ye gave me a nickel. Or two nickels."

Ted grinned. "Do ye need two nickels, boy?"

Nosey yawned. "I don't know of anyone who doesn't."

"I don't at the moment." Ted took the same two nickels he had taken earlier from Nosey's shoe and tossed them onto his lap. "Enjoy yerself."

"Well, well," the boy said with surprise. He looked quizzically into Ted's dark Irish face, with its eyes slightly too far apart, bristled black beard, and a long straight scar that ran from his right ear to just under his right eye—a bayonet wound suffered during the Battle of Gettysburg. "You're not a bad sort, after all. Are ye?"

"He can be," Rudy said with a smirk.

The two men left Nosey in the hallway. Nosey's stomach growled, as he continued picking lice from his clothes. With his ten cents, Nosey was tempted to go out and get some whiskey. Just one look at the snow, however, and he changed his mind. Anyway, he was too hungry, and there was a jug of port wine in the kitchen upstairs.

From the corner of his eye, he perceived what appeared to be an old woman hobbling through the snowflakes and making her way to the boarding house. She was weighed down by a sack of groceries. An easy target, even for Nosey. He got up and crept, like a large, shabby spider, along the wall until he got to the refuse bin. He removed a three-foot length of piano wire from his pocket.

When Katie Cunnigham opened the front door, she announced, "It's me, Nosey—your sister."

Nosey stood up. "How'd ye know I was here?"

Katie pushed her way passed him. "I saw ye from the street, ye sot. Yer about as hard to notice as a horse in a church." As she climbed the stairs, the ache in the left side of her ribs began to throb.

Nosey followed his sister. "Why the limp? I thought ye was an old hag before when I seen ye crossin' the street. And why ain't there no dress under yer coat?'

Katie sighed. "Why? Do ye care?"

Nosey followed her from the vermin-covered hallway into the vermin-covered room they shared. Their furniture consisted of a kerosene lamp, a table, two chairs, a commode, and two cots. Nosey grabbed a porcelain jar filled with port wine from under the table. He drank greedily, spilling much of it onto his chin and neck.

After Katie started the fire, she removed her coat. Nosey could see that she had been wearing only a stained bodice and petticoat beneath. "Harlot," he mumbled. "Cheap and typical stupid girl." He took another great swig from the jar.

As Katie began supper, she thought, "Two more days, Mr. Nosey Cunningham, and you can go straight to the devil." She grabbed a knife and began slicing the mold off the four-day-old bread and cheese.

"Are ye going to put on a robe, harlot?" Nosey asked. "Or are ye expectin' a man to come here? Cheat Old Cyril out of two bits, eh?"

"If ye want me to wear my robe, ye can get it for me," Katie said. She looked out the window. Even through the snow, she could see the northernmost end of the docks. "How far away is Frank?" she wondered. "The name of the whaler is the Augustus," she remembered him telling her. "I'll be coming in on the Augustus."

"Harlot," Nosey repeated. He took another gulp of port. "Do ye know that's what people call ye? They says to me, 'Nosey, how come yer not peddling yer sister's arse?' That's what they says. Is that how I brought ye up?"

Katie trimmed the last bit of mold off the bread. "How you brought me up? I guess not, my brother. Ye brought me up to go to school. Or to become a nun. Am I right? Isn't that how ye brought me up?"

Nosey wiped his mouth. "To hell with ye!" he shouted.

"Bastard," Katie mumbled.

Nosey drained the remaining port into his mouth. "Eh?"

"Eh?" Katie mimicked.

"Harlot and bitch!" he cried. He threw the jar at his sister's near-nakedness, but missed by several feet. The jar exploded in blue and white shards of porcelain against the wall.

"O, very nice!" Katie screamed. "Ye can clean that, now!"

From above, Ted's voice boomed, "Quiet that noise, down there!"

Neither Katie nor Nosey paid any heed. "Two more days," she muttered.

"Eh, what?"

"Nothing!" Katie shouted. "Nothing of your concern!"

"Right!" Nosey shouted back. "Nothing of my bloody concern! And what is *your* concern, sister? If I die of cold or from want of food, it's not Katie Cunningham's concern! Ye better show me a little more appreciation, girl. I'm tired of this sad-eyed martyr look. I got ye out of that damned orphanage! In another year, ye would've been put to work in one of them damned workhouses. Is what Cyril made ye do any worse? I suppose not. But I thought ye would be finished with this by now. Ye should've learned how to do something else by now. But ye know what I think? I think ye like what ye do and that's why yer still at it. Whore. Harlot. Am I right?"

"Aye, blessed brother," said Katie. She sliced the cheese into small cubes. It made it look like there was more cheese than there actually was when cut that way. She couldn't fool one's hunger, but maybe mislead it a bit. "Aye. I love every day of it. Maybe you should try it."

"I'll not have any of yer lip, whore! Give me my bloody supper or I swear by Christ I'll kill ye!" He picked up a tin cup and hurled it, this time accurately, at Katie's head. The jagged handle opened a small gash just behind her ear.

"Bloody hell!" Katie screamed. "Ye want yer supper? Here, then, pimp! 'cause yer no better!" She opened the window, and scraped the bread and cheese into the freezing darkness. "Go down there with the other rats and enjoy yer supper!"

Nosey jumped to his feet. "Bitch!" He pulled out his length of piano wire and stumbled to his sister.

"Help! Murder!" Katie screamed. "*Murder!*"

*   *   *

The scarred little girl, to whom Rudy had tossed the two-cent pieces from the carriage, plodded barefoot through the snow mounting on the walkways. Hannah, who was nine years old and had yet to see a bathtub, decided she was going to keep three of the thirteen cents she'd acquired from begging. She'd heard that The Hester Street Mission was selling used shoes for two-bits a pair. In little over a week, she estimated, she would have enough money to keep her feet off the ice and snow.

Hannah passed a woman with her four young children huddling around her for the warmth of her rags. They looked up to Hannah, as if to ask her for alms. But after recognizing her as one of their own kind, they cast their beaten, swollen eyes back down. It made Hannah think of her mother, but whenever she did so, she only found flickering images: a breast, tearful eyes, a chipped tooth. Hannah never knew what became of her mother.

A hand as big as her head clamped down on Hannah's shoulder and pulled her back a yard. "What have ye, rat? Little bitch, what have ye?" Hannah looked up into a grizzly, sneering face: yellow teeth sticking out in several directions, gray-brown bristle, red and green eyes. It was the face of a bogeyman, of a denizen of hell, of Hannah's father. "Tell! What have ye?" He grabbed a handful of her stringy brown hair. "Out with it!"

"Ten cents, da," Hannah said through her grimace. She held out the cigar box which held three two-cent pieces and four pennies. "Here."

Her father twisted her hand until the coins fell into his. "Ten cents," he muttered. He shook his head. "Yer out there all day and ten cents is all ye have." He backhanded her across the face. "Lazy filthy rat."

Hannah placed the palm of her hand on her stinging cheek. "I'm not lazy, da. People got no money."

Her father pummeled her face with his fist so hard she staggered back four steps into an alleyway. He followed after her. "People got money! They're out Christmas shopping! Rat!" He locked his hands together, and, as if swinging a sledgehammer, brought then down on Hannah's head. "Yer holding out on me! Bitch! Give!"

Too stunned to comprehend, Hannah reached for a wall to steady herself. But finding none, she fell.

Her father continued. "Give, little rat!" He kicked Hannah in the head. "I told you to GIVE!"

           *   *   *

Ted and Rudy sleepily plodded down the stairs. "Crazy bastards," Ted grumbled. He pulled his blue suspenders onto his shoulders.

Rudy pounded on the door. "Nosey! Katie! Let me in. It's me, Rudy Red! Come, now open the damn door!" When he didn't get a reply, he tried the handle. The door opened.

Rudy stepped into the room. He found Nosey face-down on the floor; he appeared to have passed out. "Bugger," Rudy mumbled. He walked over to Nosey. "Nosey, hey!" Rudy prodded Nosey's ribs with his toe. "C'mon, bastard, wake up!"

"Sst!" Ted signaled. "Here!"

"What?" Rudy asked.

Ted pointed to the corner of the far end of the room. "There."

Rudy looked. He saw little Katie Cunningham standing in the darkness behind the stove. He was going to step over to her when Ted restrained him.

"Look, again," Ted instructed.

Rudy then saw the reddish smears on Katie's petticoat. A blood-drenched knife quivered in her hand.

"It was an accident," Katie whispered. "Accident."

*   *   *

At The Suicide Hall, Cyril Stephens sat with Police Superintendent Michael Connery, and poured glasses of whiskey. "Tis almost the end of the year, Mike. Let's drink to the coming of 1867."

Superintendent Connery raised his glass. He did not like The Suicide Hall, but since so many of his officers drank there freely, he figured why not himself. Anyway, The Suicide Hall was all but untouchable, as most of Cyril's financing had come from members of Tweed's ring. "Aye. Let us hope we won't have another flippin' Civil War!" He brought the glass to his thick, black mustache and drank. His earlier elation about his engagement had been eclipsed by the now-confirmed impending battle between The Dead Rabbits and The Bowery Boys. And after that battle, another envelope would be forced into his hands: an envelope he did not need and did not want.

A waiter appeared at the table. "Sir, I have to talk to ye."

Cyril wiped his lips. "What is it, lad?"

"It's one of the girls, sir," the waiter said anxiously. "She said she just swallowed poison. Said she was tired of life."

Cyril smiled. "Which girl?"

"Maggie, sir." The waiter gestured with his head toward the bar.

Cyril looked over. Twenty-four years old and past her prime, Maggie Burke sat at the end of the bar, her tear-streaked face in her hands. Her torso was quivering. Already, a group of curious men were gathering around her, wondering if they'd finally see what they'd heard about the place.

"Superintendent," Cyril said, "I'll be needing your pony and trap."

"Very well," Connery said, pouring another whiskey for himself. "Just make sure I have it back before two-thirty. And, mind ye, I know nothin' about this."

Cyril waddled over to what once had been his most popular and profitable girl. Her strawberry blonde hair was soaked with sweat. The odor from her body indicated to Cyril that she had defecated. The end was near.

"Maggie," Cyril beckoned.

The young woman's hazel eyes stopped rolling and fixed themselves on Cyril. She tried to spit into his face but didn't have the strength. She breathed heavily but deliberately, in order to make sure that she could tell Cyril what she had to tell him before dying. "The Devil and I will see ye in hell, bastard," she muttered weakly.

Cyril signaled for the band to stop playing. He turned to the patrons in the smoke-filled hall. "Gentlemen! Gentlemen! Silence, please!" he yelled with raised hands. After a few more calls for silence, Cyril had the men's attention. "Thank you. The woman you see sitting beside me is Maggie Burke, formerly of County

Cork. Maggie was one of the best to ever have been in my employ. I remember her as a young girl with nowhere else to turn. She had no food in her stomach, no roof over her head, not one friend in the world. She had been at the mercy of the men she hooked in the streets, and that mercy, gentlemen, was never forthcoming. She had been treated with savagery. So I took her in.

"For some reason, however, the cruelty which had inflicted itself upon her remained within her, and now has turned upon itself. She has, alas, just now taken poison. At no extra charge, will you please join me in observation of sweet Maggie's voluntary passing from this world? Thank you."

The hall was still for several moments, except for the shuffling feet of men who needed a better view. Soon, Maggie's breathing became heavy and gurgled. Greenish-brown slime bubbled from her nostrils. She clutched her stomach.

"She's goin" a patron said. He was hushed by several men.

Maggie ceased breathing. A brown bile trickled from between her lips and onto the sawdust. The chattering of her teeth intensified and then subsided. Her eyes fixed on nothing. And then, deflated of life, Maggie Burke crumpled to the floor.

Cyril placed his hand on his heart. "Most of the girls who end up here have been on the downgrade too long to even consider reforming. I just want to say that I never pushed a girl downhill any more than I ever refused to lend a hand to one who wanted to rise. Many of these girls wished to rise—but could not. Fare thee well, Maggie. May the Lord take thee." He turned to Superintendent Connery, "Mike, will you help me here?" He then turned to the stage, "Maestro, strike up the players!" And, finally to the bartenders, "Sirs, a round for everybody—on me!"

The men cheered and tossed their hats in the air.

*   *   *

Katie Cunningham sat on a chair in her apartment, and stared blankly out the window. She hadn't stopped crying because she'd never begun.

Ted had taken the knife from her hand and washed it clean of blood. Rudy Red, meanwhile, continued standing with his fists on his hips over the corpse of Nosey. Finally, he asked, "What are we to do, Ted? It was an accident, after all. The bloody fool goes to murder his sister with wire and runs into her knife."

Ted wiped the knife dry and placed it into a drawer. He scratched his black beard. "We can't very well call for the police."

"Why not?" Rudy asked. "Twas an accident. Or self-defense."

Ted walked over to Rudy and joined him in the vigil. "And what lawyer would take the case from a woman who cannot pay for his services? And what jury would believe that a prostitute, whose brother sold her to The Suicide Hall, did not have a motive for killing him? And what judge would not consider sending her to Bedloe's Island?"

"I shall hang from the gallows." Katie mumbled softly. She turned to her brother's body. "Another thing I have to thank ye for, Nosey. Just like the way you brought me up." She looked up at the two men, then she laughed. "Do ye know that's what he said to me? He said, 'Why are ye still a whore? I didn't bring ye up that way.' He sold me to that pimp!" The tears finally escaped from the corners of her eyes, and, like fugitives, they traveled quickly over a long distance. "I was only thirteen years old!" She added bitterly, "The way he brought me up!"

Ted muttered, "The dopey dead bastard."

Katie returned her attention to the window. "I shall be hanged," she repeated.

"Nonsense," Rudy said. "I'll not hear of it."

"Aye," Ted said, with a nod. "Nobody deserves to be punished for ridding the world of that stupid sot. I refuse to allow that!"

"First thing ye do, Katie," Rudy began, "is burn those bloodied clothes. Those can be evidence in a murder charge."

Katie nodded her head. "Aye. And what do I do with him? Burn him, too?"

Ted shook his head. "No. Don't worry about Nosey. I have an idea."

Katie wasn't listening. She kept staring at the docks in the distance. Frank would be here in two days, "But now this. He won't take me away. How can he make me his wife? A murderess," she thought. Every time a vision of Frank materialized in her mind, it would be overshadowed by one of Nosey rushing at her with the wire. "I'm glad you're dead," she said mentally to the specter.

"Katie," Ted called. "Girl, I'm not worried about the bed-clothes, the knife or the body. I'm worried about *you*. If ye want to stay away from the gallows, ye had better heed what I tell ye. Yer miserable brother ruined what few years ye had. Don't let him ruin the ones ye have coming to ye. But if yer conscience can't bear it, maybe it's best we call the police. Because we don't want to join ye at the hanging grounds for being accessories."

"What?" Rudy asked. "We hang, too?"

Ted nodded gravely.

Katie looked up with a surprised expression. "What are ye saying, then? Ye think we can really get away with it?"

"That's what I'm saying. But, when it's all over and done with, ye must leave the city."

Rudy, still stunned by the possibility of capital punishment finding his neck, said, "She can't leave. Cyril would track her down. No girl leaves The Suicide Hall, unless she's killed herself."

"I know," Ted replied. "I'll think of something."

"Cyril can't track me to Iceland" Katie interjected.

"Iceland?" Rudy asked.

"I'm going to Iceland," Katie said. "In two days."

"How is that?" Ted asked.

She looked into Ted's eyes. "I have a lover. His name is Frank. He's on a whaling ship right now that's going to dock here on Friday. The Augustus. He's going to take me away to Iceland. That is his home. He loves me and I don't doubt that. Many men have promised to take me away but I never believed them. But Frank, he will take me away."

"Are ye sure?" Rudy asked.

Ted smiled. "She's sure. But we must have an alternative. Just in case."

Katie returned the smile, and looked back to the docks.

"Let's get started, then," Rudy advised, feeling he didn't want to be in the room any longer with the corpse. "Now, what to do with our dearly departed friend here?"

Ted pulled a bed sheet from Nosey's cot. "He won't be needing this, anymore." He spread the sheet out on the floor. "Don't look, Katie." When he saw that the girl continued staring out the window, he rolled the body onto the sheet. Blood spilled from Nosey's mouth. The expression on the open-eyed corpse was one of mild surprise, as if he were going to say, "Bloody hell, I'm dead!"

Rudy assisted with wrapping the body in the sheet. After that, the two carried Nosey out into the hallway and up the stairs to the roof. The snow was still falling though not as ferociously as earlier. Gas lamps dotted the cityscape around them. Not too far off in the distance the black spires of St. Paul's and Trinity churches tolled the late hour.

"There by the chimney," Ted instructed, indicating the area of the roof most covered by snowdrifts. They buried Nosey under one such drift, and packed more snow atop, but not before Ted took back the two nickels from the corpse's shoe.

"We're not going to just leave him under there, are we?" Rudy asked. "He'll stink the whole building when he thaws."

Ted rubbed his chapped hands together. "Nay. If my guess is right, there will be a war tomorrow between The Dead Rabbits and The Bowery Boys. We just come up and get Nosey, and put him in the street with the other bodies. Just another stab victim. Now, let's go in. It's bloody cold."

Rudy restrained him. "Hang on," he said, smiling. "I may not be the brightest of men, but I do know *you*. Why are ye really doing this? What do ye care whether Katie Cunningham goes to Bedloe's Island or not? There's money in it, isn't there?"

Ted wrapped his arms across his chest. "Nosey Cunningham was shite—nothing more, nothing less. I hated the sot from head to foot. Every time I looked at him, I would ask myself, 'Is this why I left Ireland? Is this the kind of person I went to fight the confederacy for while he burned the Negro orphanage during the Draft Riots?' When the so-called "True Americans" think of the Irish, do they think of him or do they think of me? Katie did something I wish I had done. And I won't see that child suffer because of this little shite." Ted headed for the doorway. "And, beside," he added, "there might be some money in this, too."

*   *   *

Katie Cunningham stood naked in front of the stove. She wrapped her bloodied bodice and petticoat around chunks of wood, and tossed it into the fire. She pulled up a chair, and sat with her elbows on her knees and her head in her hands.

"I don't feel bad," she thought. "I don't feel guilty."

She watched the materials pop in the flames. White ashes ascended into the chimney pipe, traveled to the roof, and out into the snow flurry.

"I feel nothing."

Outside, in the East River, a ship blasted its foghorn. Its long, mournful sound caught Katie's attention. And she smiled.

*   *   *

Fired by his inordinate consumption of alcohol and the penumbra of a large-scale gang war, Superintendent of Police Michael Connery bowed under the weight of his dark gray cloud of doubt. Sitting on his bed in his brownstone apartment, he watched with disinterest the light traffic of suspicious carriages and empty yellow omnibuses rolling through the intersection of Fifth Avenue and 32nd Street.

Certainly, the next day's battle in the muddy gutters of The Five Points would neither be the first nor the last with which he would have to contend. The same could be said of the envelope full of cash that Petey Daley will give him for turning his back on the incident. As much as it nauseated him with indignation, Connery had come to accept this necessity.

"But would a wife accept it?" he wondered. He thought of his fiancée. "What would Elizabeth think, seeing me come home with all that money? And if I don't show it to her, how do I hide it? I'm probably the only man in the bloody country who worries about such things but…She believes me to be an honest officer of the law who saved her from injustice. Should she ever discover that I am as bad as her accuser…God." He sighed deeply, lay down on his back, and clasped his hands behind his head. "And, if I do hide the money, how do I explain where it came from when an expense comes around—like a child? I will not deny our child anything for want of money!"

He reached for the pillow and put it under his head. His feet dangled over the side of the bed. "No good will come from hiding the money. No good," he decided. Thus he was brought back to his original question. "What would Elizabeth think, seeing me with all that extra cash?"

Connery scratched the dinner crumbs out of his mustache. He came to the conclusion that he would not sleep well that night, and he didn't.

*   *   *

Hermann Graebel gently wiped off the stains of bile on the front of Maggie Burke's bodice. With a wooden comb, he pulled her hair away from her face. The old caretaker treated the corpse as if she were his own young daughter on her way to meet her first suitor. "Now, it's bad enough that you are going where you are going dressed like a tart, but at least you can be a clean tart." He took a step back and regarded the corpse in the coffin. "Ach, so young."

Hermann had never been to The Suicide Hall but felt he knew it well. Corpses of the girls who'd worked there, as well as belligerent customers, wound up in his shack often enough. And Hermann's friend, Officer Cavanaugh, frequented the place whenever he succumbed to his desires for the flesh. The young officer often confessed to Hermann about his occasional visits to the brothel. These confessions eased the burden of Cavanaugh's guilty conscience, forged there by his Catholic upbringing.

"You poor girls," Hermann sighed. He was quick to add, "But what choice did you have? Starvation?" He re-laced Maggie's bodice. "So much of your life spent on your back. And now you must spend all eternity that way." He scanned his shack until his eyes fell upon a small beaten cushion. He reached out and then gently placed it under Maggie's head. "There. At least I can make it a little more comfortable for you."

After some final preening, Old Hermann reached for the lid of the casket. But before nailing it on, he made a gesture of warning with his forefinger. "Now, wherever it is you're going, do not be ashamed of anything you may have done in this world. There is no reason to be ashamed, young lady. It is said Mary Magdelene was like you before she met Jesus—and look what became of her! You're in good company." He placed the lid on the pine box and reached for his hammer and some nails. Under his breath, he added, "If you believe in such things."

*   *   *

The first cries were heard shortly after dawn. Six hundred boys and men raced up the snow-covered street calling for Petey Daley and his blood. They carried clubs, slung-shots, knives, brickbats, pipes, and planks of wood. Forty of them brandished Confederate swords. One carried a revolver. Although armed for war, they were still dressed in style: black cravats, wide-lapelled jackets and black stove pipe hats. These were The Bowery Boys.

"Come out, sons of bitches!" and "Death for you bastards!" they hollered.

From the window of their apartment, Rudy and Ted watched the mob gather in front of the building on the corner of Orange and Cross Streets—the headquarters of The Dead Rabbits.

"It'll be war," Rudy noted.

"Stupid arses, "Ted said.

Rocks and bottles were tossed at the doorway of The Dead Rabbits' headquarters. "We want our food! Give us our coal!" they demanded. "Come out, Petey!" A shot was fired at the building. "Death to the papists!" The closed doors and windows only emphasized The Rabbits' indifference.

"I can't understand why Petey doesn't come out and fight," Rudy said.

Ted shrugged.

"Bastard, come out! Fight like a man, ye little shite," yelled Terry Billings, the leader of The Bowery Boys. "Come on, Wee Petey! Come out!"

The chant went up, "Wee Petey! Wee Petey! Wee Petey!"

Ted nudged Rudy, "Get ready. It has to come now."

A window on the lowest floor of The Rabbits' headquarters went up. Tattered brown curtains flapped in the wind. The Bowery Boys ceased their taunting and looked expectantly at the window. The street was silent.

"Ho, Wee Petey," Terry Billings called. "Have you something to say, you little coward?"

In response, the barrel of a cannon protruded from the window. The entire block shook as it was set off. The cannonball roared across the street and crashed into the side of a shanty, but not before it had torn nearly unimpeded through six Bowery Boys and ripped off the arm of a seventh.

"JAY-zus!" Rudy exclaimed.

Ted shook his head, "Stupid, stupid bastards."

The Dead Rabbits, with Petey Daley leading the way, poured out of the doors and windows of their headquarters. Petey held an eight-foot pole with a dagger tied to the end. With this makeshift spear, he immediately stabbed four Bowery Boys. The burly Black Roger, hired as a bodyguard and hired muscle, swung a four-foot length of lead pipe to keep the Bowery Boys off Petey's back.

Other members of The Dead Rabbits swung meat cleavers, clubs, and lengths of chain. With red stripes sewn onto the outer seams of their trousers, The Dead Rabbits looked more like an organized army than The Bowery Boys.

The cannon shot was not only an offensive maneuver; it was a signal to The Roach Guard—temporarily allied with The Rabbits—to join the fray. Three hundred Roach Guard, armed with iron bars and wooden clubs, rushed to battle from every alleyway.

From their window, Rudy and Ted watched the carnage. The streets and walks reddened with every passing minute. Another shot was fired that grazed Petey Daley on the neck.

"Petey's been hit!" Rudy yelled.

Ted laughed. "Just gives him more incentive to fight."

Indeed, Petey, after seeing that his blood was drawn, returned the favor and stuck his spear into the gunman's throat.

"Why do ye want yer meat back?" Black Roger cried. "Ye ain't goin' to be able to chew it!" To emphasize his point, he rapped his pipe across the mouths of two Bowery Boys.

Petey Daley noticed that one of the youngest members of his gang, the hare-lipped Max, was sitting on the ground, his back against a wall. "Up with ye, Max," Petey said. "Don't fear! Come, boy." He grabbed the teen by his collar and yanked him up. When he did so, he saw the back of the boy's skull and some brain tissue cling to the wall, where his head had been dashed. "Bloody bastards!" Petey screamed. He saw Terry Billings standing dazed at the periphery of the battle—his face was covered with blood. "Billings!" he cried.

Terry Billings heard the call and saw the diminutive Petey with the long spear charging toward him. Billings turned and fled.

"Here comes the mighty Terry," Rudy Red mused, as Terry Billings ran beneath their window. Long-legged Terry had no trouble outrunning the stocky Petey. Breathless, Wee Petey stopped running in front of the boarding house. He called out, "Yer a dead man, Terry! A dead man!"

Ted threw open the window and hollered, "Petey! Mind yer back!"

Petey looked up at Ted, and then spun around. One of the sword-bearing Bowery Boys had been creeping up behind him. Petey stuck his spear into the Boy's chest. Once the Boy fell, Petey straddled him and dug his spear several times into his torso. He only stopped when the blade snapped off. Done, Petey wiped the sweat and blood from his brow. He looked up and called to Ted, "I owe you one, friend!" Then Petey winked, picked up the Boy's sword, and ran back to the battle.

*   *   *

What had prevented skinny little Hannah from freezing to death was the simple fact that she had fallen unconscious next to a grate from which steam had escaped during the night. The snow had stopped then, too. The alleyway she lay in had been warmed by the sun in the cloudless sky. Her head and ribs were sore when she awoke. She tried to stand but could only crawl. Then she sat down again. She rubbed her head again.

A few feet away rats were rummaging through a refuse bin. She crawled toward it and found some chicken bones. Banging the side of the bin with her tiny fist, she frightened away some of the rats; the rest hardly budged from their feasting. But there was enough room for her grab a few bones. She eagerly devoured some of the gristle before she tossed everything aside. She rubbed her side, "Ow-w-w." Her other hand grabbed a fistful of snow which she also munched on and devoured. There was no need for her to check her drawers; she knew her father had taken the three pennies she had hidden in them.

After massaging her head and ribs again, she managed to stand. An unknown source of energy had propelled her forward—to start walking away. Tiny drops of blood from her feet dotted her trail. She didn't know where she was going to go, just some place far away from the man she had called, "Pa." And although she felt she had walked for miles, she found herself on Baxter Street, just a few blocks away.

A curious boy, maybe a few years older than Hannah, but many pounds heavier, leaned on a small crate in front of 24 Baxter Street or, rather, what was left of 24 Baxter Street. It was a small, grey house with a severely sloped roof from which two arched dormers protruded. Three steps lead to the front door. Once upon a time it might have been considered a handsome home but for years it had not been. The chimney between the dormers had long since collapsed; some of the bricks still rested on the weather worn shingles. The windows of the dormers had been blown out by a fire in the attic several years earlier. The four other windows—two on the ground floor and two on the floor above—were boarded over, and the shutters hung at odd angles beside them. The stone slabs which had formed the steps were severely chipped and worn. One of the black cast-iron handrails leaned in toward the steps; the other was missing completely. The alleyway alongside the building was strewn with broken bottles and crates of refuse. It was one of those types of crates upon which the heavy-set boy leaned. There was a crude, hand-painted sign on the crate which read, "Cut-Throats! 4 cents." But Hannah could not read the sign. "Do you want to see it?" the pudgy boy asked. "Do you want to come in?"

Hannah nodded.

"Then show me the four cents," the boy, Baby-Face Neeley, demanded.

"Four cents?"

"If you don't have the four-cents, how do you expect to see it?" Baby-Face asked. But then he looked closely at girl. He regarded her bluish-white skin and the caked blood between her toes. "You don't know who we are, do you? Do you know where you are?"

Hannah shook her head. "I am where?"

"It's alright, little girl. Don't worry. When was the last time you ate or sat next to a fire? You're cold and you need something to eat. Am I right?" he asked.

Hannah heard the question but could not respond.

"Come on inside," Baby-Face whispered, leading the girl into 24 Baxter Street. "I'll get you some food and some stockings or something. Come on."

"I am where?" Hannah asked.

*   *   *

Outnumbered and ill-prepared, The Bowery Boys eventually scattered. The battle which normally would have lasted hours, was exhausted in only forty minutes. Scores of bodies—some dead, most were wounded, from both sides—littered the street. Rudy and Ted stood on the roof of their building and observed the neighborhood people. Old women huddled around the bodies and wept openly: some knew the people they mourned, most did not. Little children stood open-mouthed; a few of them ventured to touch and poke a body. Other children and teens rummaged through the pockets of the corpses, hoping for money or weapons.

"Come, then," Ted instructed. He and Rudy Red plodded across the roof to where they had buried Nosey. Rudy took his broom and prepared to sweep off the snow. With the first stroke, however, a half dozen rats raced from under the drift.

Ted jumped back a foot. "Bloody hell!" he hollered. "Bastards!"

Rudy laughed. "It's just me friends. Sorry if they gave ye a fright."

"Buggers!" Ted rasped.

Rudy swept away the layers of snow until he got to the bed sheet. There were holes on it where the rats had eaten through. "Is anyone looking?" Rudy asked.

Ted looked over the edge of the roof. "No. Let's be quick."

Rudy removed the sheet. Most of Nosey's face had been eaten away by the rats and the wound in his stomach had been enlarged by the gorging. "Ye look like hell, Nosey," Rudy laughed.

"Come, now," Ted admonished.

Rudy grabbed the corpse by the ankles, and dragged it to the edge of the roof. Ted grabbed Nosey's shirt collar. They lifted the corpse.

Ted took one final glance. Everyone's attention was up the street toward The Dead Rabbits' headquarters. Fortunately for the pair, nobody was paying any mind to the fallen Bowery Boy that Petey Daley had nearly eviscerated in front of the boarding house. Up the street, Ted could see the policemen's wagons approaching. "Now," Ted urged. "Hurry."

They lifted the corpse and dropped it down the narrow alley between their boarding house and the shanty next door. The body landed feet-first on a snow bank. The upper portion of it fell onto the walkway.

Rudy and Ted crossed themselves piously. Then they spat down upon Nosey's corpse.

✶   ✶   ✶

Katie Cunningham sat at the bar in The Suicide Hall, and sipped a glass of water. Everyone was talking about the gang war which had taken place.

"I hear hunnerts of boys got kilt," said one customer.

A West Indian man added, "Them boys are crazy. Used a cannon, you know." He then spat into a dented cuspidor.

But Katie hardly heard any of these exchanges. She sat cross-legged and stared into the sawdust. She thought about Rudy and Ted, and hoped they had gotten rid of her brother's corpse. "Useless bugger," she mumbled. It had never occurred to her fully how much she had hated Nosey. And, now, she knew why she felt no remorse.

As children in the orphanage, they had been separated for the most part. When they did interact, he hardly acknowledged her, except when they planned to run away. Once in the street, they slept on piles of hay by the west side docks. Katie remembered the day Nosey interrupted her nap, and waved seven dollars in her face. "Listen, Katie," he had said, "a man has given me money. He has given us a place to live. But ye must work for him." "The man" was Cyril Stephens. "Work" meant prostitution. She remembered the pain of the first man. "Useless bloody bugger!" she growled.

One of the other employees, Cynthia Stuart, a Welsh girl, sat next to Katie. A complete contrast to Katie, Cynthia was tall, blonde, thin lipped, and had nearly transparent blue eyes. One of her top teeth had been punched out some weeks earlier by a customer. "Katie, did you hear about Maggie?"

Katie, startled out of her reverie, looked up. "Eh? Cynthia?"

"Maggie!" Cynthia exclaimed in a whisper. "She took poison last night."

"Maggie Burke?" Katie asked.

"Yes!" Cynthia replied. She brushed away a lock of her. "Right here at the bar."

"Dead?"

"Can't get any more dead," Cynthia answered.

"She's the fourth one this year, " Katie muttered. She sipped her water again. She thought, "And if Frank doesn't come tomorrow, I shall be the fifth."

Cyril waddled over, brushing cigar ashes from his plaid jacket. "Girls, how are you?"

"Fine," Cynthia said. "Have you got some work for me?"

Cyril smiled. "In fact, I've work for you both." He gave Cynthia and Katie two bits each. "Cynthia, love, room 2. Katie, dear, room 5. Nice boys. No problem, eh?"

"Wasn't it a nice boy that punched Cynthia in the mouth?" Katie asked. She got up and headed toward the stairway.

Although it would hardly seem possible, Cyril's eyes bulged further. "Now, Katie!"

Cynthia grabbed the pimp's elbow. "Let her alone. She's just heard about Maggie and she's very upset."

Cyril continued glaring in Katie's direction. "Aye," he said. Then he turned to Cynthia, "Up with you, girl, room 2."

Cynthia followed Katie up the stairs.

Cyril removed a soiled handkerchief from his pocket and wiped his forehead. He turned to the bartender. "Let's have a whiskey."

*   *   *

Police Superintendent Michael Connery knocked on the door of the building on the corner of Cross and Orange Streets. His men inspected the corpses that were strewn about. One new officer vomited upon seeing and smelling the carnage.

Petey Daley opened the door of The Dead Rabbits Headquarters. There was a gauze bandage wrapped around his neck. "Afternoon, Superintendent."

"Afternoon, Petey," Connery said. He rubbed his finger along his mustache.

Petey smiled. "Is there something I can do for ye?"

Connery shrugged. "Perhaps." He turned and watched his men pile the bodies onto a cart. "I just want to tell ye that we're just here to clean up the area. We aren't looking to arrest anyone."

"Understood," Petey said. "Terrible thing that happened here." He handed the Superintendent an envelope.

"Aye," said Connery. "Listen, son, I have request of ye."

Petey looped his thumbs around his black suspenders. "Perhaps I can oblige."

"Perhaps ye can," Connery said. "Tis as simple as this: ye don't want me coming into this neighborhood, and my men don't want to come here."

"And?" Petey asked.

Connery sighed. "All I ask of you and yer men, is that the next time something like this happens—and even though I am well aware that you have nothing to do with these awful rows—would ye leave the bodies somewhere outside the area? Like on Pearl Street?"

Petey nodded." Aye, Superintendent. Tis reasonable."

"Thank ye, Petey." Connery tipped his hat. He braced his collar against the wind. "Tis damp, son. Best I let ye back inside. Take care of that nick on yer neck. Good day to ye."

"Good day, superintendent," Petey said, as he closed the door.

Within ten minutes, the officers, under Superintendent Connery's barking orders, had whisked away most of the bodies.

Rudy and Ted drank cups of tea, and observed the clean-up from their window. The last body to be tossed onto a cart was that of Nosey Cunningham.

The officers looked curiously at the corpse. They noticed it was bluer than the other victims. The bites on its face were unlike the human bite marks on the others and something, it appeared, had tried to eat the contents of its stomach. The two officers looked at each other, and then shrugged. They climbed onto the riding seats and put the whip to the horse. Soon, they were gone.

Rudy and Ted clinked their teacups together.

*　　　　　　*　　　　　　*

After feasting on mutton and potatoes, Ted and Rudy strolled uptown. Rudy donned the same upper class outfit he'd worn the day before when he'd sold the Brumaire. The only exception was that this time he sported a walking stick. Ted wore a simple, bright green waistcoat and carried an Irish newspaper under his arm. Concealed in his vest pocket was a single-shot pistol.

At dusk, the temperature actually had begun to rise, and the wind abated considerably. People were in the streets for their evening constitutions, something which they had been denied during the snowstorm of the previous night. Coaches raced along 23rd Street, hurrying their customers to theaters. The gaslights were just being lit to guide everyone under the gold and purple dusk.

On 24th Street, the pair found a pub that was not too crowded, O'Molloy's. Ted entered first. He placed his newspaper on the bar and ordered a pint of stout. As he sipped his thick, dark drink, he made a quick inventory of the establishment. He found the one thing he wanted to find: a dart board. He didn't see the one thing that he didn't want to see: police. He strolled to the door, opened it, and peeked outside, as if he were expecting someone. He spat on the pavement as a signal to Rudy that the coast was clear. He put his hands in his pockets and returned to the bar.

"Excuse me, sir," Ted called to the bartender. "May I play a game of darts?"

The bartender, a middle-aged man with thinning hair, waved his hand apathetically, telling Ted he could do whatever he pleased with the dart board.

"Thank ye," Ted said.

As Ted tossed a few practice shots, the handsome Rudy Red entered the pub, and twirled his walking stick. He paused to observe Ted's play.

"Can I get ye something, sir?" the bartender asked.

Once more twirling the stick, Rudy stepped up to the bar. In a heavy British accent, Rudy said, "I'm a bit early for the theater and I thought I would treat myself to a cordial. Let's have a gin!" He placed a few coins on the bar.

Ted tossed two cork-shots.

"Bloody lucky," Rudy laughed. As the bartender gave Rudy his change and gin, Rudy said, "The gentleman fancies himself a dart player." For a few more moments, he watched Ted: more cork-shots and a few misses.

While the bartender poured Rudy another gin, Rudy called out to Ted, "Well, well, if I'm not witnessing the blessed luck of the Irish!" Then he laughed.

One of the patrons, a tired-eyed dock worker, called out, "Mind yer lip, ye English bastard."

Ted turned around and said to Rudy, "Aye, watch yer lip."

Rudy put up his hand, "Gentlemen, gentlemen, I meant no offense. Please, pardon me." He removed a dollar from his pocket and placed it on the bar. "In fact, bartender, as a gesture of good-will, please buy these good men a drink from me."

The dockworker responded, "I don't want anything from that English Nancy-boy." Several other patrons declined, as well. Only those who were long on thirst but short on money accepted.

When Rudy had finished his fourth gin, he called to Ted, "Here, friend, how about a game of darts? You and me?"

Ted kept his back to the bar.

"Come!" Rudy cried. "Here. We'll make it interesting." Rudy grabbed his hat and tossed in two dollars. "Come, now."

Ted looked into the hat. He curled his lip. "I don't play with limeys."

"Oh, now, calling me names, are we?" Rudy asked. "I did not call any of you people a name. My comment about 'Luck of the Irish' might have been in poor taste, I admit, but I did not mean it derogatorily."

Ted looked Rudy in the eyes, and then nodded. "Very well then." He reached into his pocket and placed his own two dollars into the hat. "What shall we play until? Seven points?"

Rudy nodded. "Seven points, it is. Shall I start then?"

"Aye, sir," Ted smiled.

The two held the interest of about a half dozen patrons—all of them rooting for 'Irish' Ted. But it wasn't much of a game. Ted had beaten Rudy soundly: 7-4.

The best Rudy had succeeded in doing was not fall over every time he went for a cork-shot. He stumbled to the bar and ordered another gin. He said to the bartender, "I say, he is a good dart player." Reaching into his hat he gave Ted the winnings. "I must admit honestly that you're a better player than I, sir. Here's your money."

Ted put up his hands. "Keep it, you stumble-drunk. I don't want yer bloody English money. I just wanted to teach ye a lesson: next time yer too sotted to know what yer doin', keep yer fool mouth closed." He grabbed his original two dollars from Rudy's hand and pocketed it.

Rudy stood dumbfounded for a few moments. Then, he said, "Teach me a bloody lesson? O. I like that!" Rudy exclaimed. "Sir! I like that! My money's not good enough? My English money? Here!" He tossed a ten-dollar bill into his hat. "C'mon then! Teach me a lesson, again! I failed your test! Come now, man!"

"Bugger off," Ted sighed.

Rudy's face reddened. "I shan't, good sir!" He waved the hat in front of Ted's face. "Come on! I admitted that you're a good dart player, but you're not *that* good! I can beat your Irish hide! Come, now, put up!"

Rudy's comment about Ted's Royal Irish Hide caused a stir among the patrons. The dock worker called to Ted, "Go ahead, friend, take the bloody Orangeman's money. You'll beat him again! Here, I got two dollars says you can!" He tossed the bills into the hat.

"Very well," Rudy approved. "And here, sir, are my two dollars, as a show of good faith." He flashed two dollars and placed it into the hat. "Any others? Don't be shy!"

Several patrons gathered around Rudy and stuffed his hat with dollars, which, for each and every one, Rudy matched. When he saw that the customers who wanted to wager did, he turned to Ted. "And, now, you sir...What say you?"

Ted looked around the pub: the eager eyes of the patrons urged him to bet and play. "Very well, sir." The crowd cheered as Ted tossed his ten dollars into the hat.

The game started with Ted running up a 3-0 lead. Every time he moved to the side to allow Rudy to shoot, he got an occasional pat on the back from a customer.

Rudy wiped the sweat from his forehead. Speaking to himself (although making sure the others heard), Rudy muttered, "Straighten up, man. You have a lot of money to lose."

"Aye, that he does," the dockworker said to his friend.

Rudy took a deep breath, and tossed two corkers out of three: the score was 3-2, in favor of Ted.

"Ye still have the lead, man," a customer called out to Ted. "Don't let him intimidate ye."

But Ted made sure he showed signs of intimidation. He nervously tugged at his collar and adjusted his shirt cuff. He glanced around him. He tossed one corker out of three: 4-2, Ted.

"That's it," the dockworker said. "Slow and easy!"

Before playing, Rudy asked the bartender for a glass of water.

"C'mon," Ted admonished. "Play!"

A patron whispered to Ted, "Don't incite him, friend. Let him have his water."

Rudy put down his glass and thanked the bartender. He stepped up to the line and, after taking careful aim, tossed three corkers. Now the score was in Rudy's favor, 5-4.

The pub, as if witnessing the Grim Reaper's entrance, went still.

Ted grabbed the darts and stepped up. He drew a breath. The first toss was a corker. A cheer went up for the tied score.

Ted acknowledged the crowd's support with a quick nod. He smiled confidently, but his next two tosses, though very close, missed the mark.

With the score tied at five, Rudy inspected the darts and approached the line. He took aim and tossed a perfect corker. One more and he would win. He gripped the second dart, aimed, and almost missed the board completely. This sent up a mild, though nervous, laugh in the pub.

Rudy's tongue rested on his lower lip. He squinted, and gracefully, perfectly, tossed the winning corker. A general groan went up in the room.

He went to shake Ted's hand. "Good game, sir."

Ted didn't accept it.

After shrugging, Rudy put five dollars on the bar and ordered drinks for the house. This time, the patrons did not refuse. A few even congratulated him on a game well-played.

"He cheated, " Ted said.

The dockworker asked, "What's that?"

Ted walked up to Rudy. "Ye cheated, ye bastard. Yer foot was over the line."

"It certainly was not!" Rudy said. "Now, look here, you lost fairly."

Ted went to grab the hat but Rudy pulled it away. "I want my money back. Ye cheat!"

"Now, sir," the bartender admonished, "I watched the whole game. His foot never went beyond the legal..."

"It did," Ted insisted.

Rudy nervously grabbed the cash, and stuffed it in his pocket. He picked up his walking stick. "I can see I'm not welcome here, gentlemen. If you'll excuse me..." Rudy, with little resistance, made his way to the exit, and left.

The dockworker pulled a stool over for Ted to sit on. "Rest yourself, friend. It's done."

Ted sulked over his now warmer stout. After a few sips, he said. "I shall track the cheat down and kill him. He took forty-two dollars from us!"

A patron advised him, "An Irishman like you, attacks an Englishman like him...ye know what would happen."

"I don't care." Ted removed his pistol. "I'm going to kill him."

Upon seeing the gun, the crowd backed away from Ted. He slowly and calmly walked to the exit.

After a few moments, a dockworker asked the bartender. "Do ye think we should go after the lad and stop him?"

Another concerned patron added, "He was incensed. He may kill you, should ye try to stop him."

"Call the coppers!" someone else offered.

"Nay!" the bartender shouted. "Leave it be! If the authorities find out that whatever happened out there happened because of in here, it will kill business."

The patrons stood about dumbly.

The bartender instructed, "Now, drink up, boys. Ye still have cocktails coming from the gentleman. Whether he's deceased or not."

*　　　　　*　　　　　*

A brown shoe dangled loosely from Hannah's left foot, a black wool sock warmed her right one. She sat munching on pickles and a wedge of three-day-old bread, in the windowless basement of 24 Baxter Street. She watched a dozen boys nail planks of grey wood into the exposed brick and stone wall behind the stage to create the illusion of a fence in an alleyway. Two girls with straw brooms swept the wings. A boy and a girl mended a hole in a tattered bed sheet which served as a curtain for the stage. There was a second theater, in the lot behind house, but that was only used during warm weather.

Hannah had offered to help—to do anything at all—but was told by Baby-Face Neeley to just relax, watch the rehearsal, and give him any thoughts she might have.

The troupe's premiere actor—the slight, fair-haired Simon Bristol—knelt before one of the larger actors on the stage. The larger boy did not wear a child's cap; instead he wore an adult's stovepipe hat. Simon begged, "O, papa, please do not punish me! I was set upon by a thief who took your money for the tankard of ale you wanted. There was nothing I could do!"

The larger boy "kicked" Simon further down. "I don't believe you! You are a thieving little bastard like your mama was! Now I'll learn you a lesson!" The larger boy removed his belt and swung at Simon. A stagehand in the wings slapped a saddle with a flat piece of wood to make it sound like Simon had been struck.

"Pa, please don't hit me no more," Simon emoted. "I swear to the Good Lord Jesus there was nothing to be done about it!"

"O, no?" the larger actor asked. "If you want me to stop hitting you, then you had better go out into the cold, cold streets and beg for money. And don't come back until you have my tankard of ale." He kicked Simon, sending him offstage.

Baby-Face leapt up from his crate, and clapped his hands. "Excellent!" He continued applauding. "Good show, Simon, Reggie!" The larger actor, Reggie, tipped his stovepipe hat. Simon, beaming with self-satisfaction, emerged from the wings and said, "Thank you."

Baby-Face tucked his copy of the script in the crook of his arm and walked over to Hannah. "See? That's what we do—put on shows. What did you think?"

Hannah's brow knit with confusion. "I don't know." She bit into the bread and looked down at her covered feet. "I guess I don't understand."

"Don't understand what? The boy is beaten by his father for losing the beer money. I think it's a good, scary scene."

"It's not real," Hannah remarked humbly.

Baby-Face smiled. "Of course it isn't real. It's acting."

Hannah shrugged. "The boy should be whipped more."

"What's that?"

"The boy should be whipped more. The way my pa whipped me."

"How so?"

Hannah put down the chunk of stale bread and swallowed the remaining pickle in her mouth. She walked toward the stage, was about to climb onto it, and then asked Baby-Face, "Can I show you?"

Amused, Baby-Face said, "Go on. Simon get down and beg again."

"Yes, Baby-Face," Simon replied, somewhat doubtfully. He knelt before Hannah who took the strap from Reggie. The stage-hand poised his plank of wood over the saddle.

Simon began, "O, papa, please do not punish me! I was..." But Simon was interrupted by a sharp kick to the abdomen by Hannah's shod foot. "Ow!"

"I don't believe ye, little rat! Where's me money?" Hannah brought the belt down twice on Simon's legs.

"Youch! Hey!" Simon cried.

"Little bitch! Rat! What have ye, then? Holding out on me? Where's the money?" The belt cracked down on Simon's back. The stagehand had difficulty synchronizing his slaps on the saddle with Hannah's fierce whips. "Rat! Rat! I want me drink! Give! Give! I want me money!"

"Ow! Help me!" Simon screamed.

"Grab her!" someone yelled.

In mid-swipe, Reggie wrapped his arms around Hannah's waist from behind and lifter her. Hannah continued thrashing and kicking. "Rat! Rat!" she shrieked, tears flying off her cheeks. And then, suddenly, she let out a long, terrible howl of misery that was insufficient to describe her nine years of wretchedness. When the cry was over, seconds later, her body went limp. The belt dropped from her hand. Reggie regarded the life-size rag doll in his arms, and then he laid her down on the stage.

After moments of silence, someone finally asked, "Is she dead?"

Reggie bent over the girl and heard her breathing. "No. She ain't dead." He listened again. "I think she's fainted."

Simon peeked out from between his forearms which were protecting his head. Seeing that the scrawny little girl had really fainted, he slowly got to his feet. He turned to Baby-Face and gasped, "She is mad. Baby-Face, she is crazy."

But Baby-Face remained transfixed where he stood, his mouth in a wide-open smile of near ecstasy. He finally blinked. "Shh, let her sleep." He stepped closer to the stage and listened to her shallow but quick breathing. He brushed her hair away from her face.

"We can't keep her here," Simon warned. "She's wild." He rubbed a welt on his thigh. "Crazy."

Baby-Face nodded. "But she's amazing!" he whispered, not taking his eyes off the girl. "Amazing. Amazing. I never seen anything so amazing." He quickly scurried to pick up the pages of the script that he'd let fall to the ground during Hannah's display. "I must rewrite the scene. I must. Reggie, can you do it the way she done?" He didn't wait for an answer. "Amazing!"

*   *   *

Two dresses, five sets of undergarments, and a pair of boots were all that Katie possessed to put into her carpetbag. The money she had saved away in a stocking leg—23 dollars in singles—was rolled up and tucked into a side compartment of the bag. She grabbed a needle and thread and prepared to seal the compartment.

Outside a church bell clanged ten times. "I'll not sleep tonight. I know it." Her stomach had been quivering all night and her thoughts kept gravitating toward the next day's voyage with Frank. Warm anticipation refused to let go of her chest.

Done with her sewing, Katie felt an urge to pray. She knelt down and began a "Hail Mary". Half-way through, however, she realized she'd forgotten the rest. She remained kneeling anyway, until there was a knock on the door. When she answered, Rudy Red was standing there, twirling a walking stick.

"Hello, Katie," Rudy said. "Ready for tomorrow?"

Katie smiled. "Aye. Everything is packed. Are ye sure the plan will work?"

Rudy smiled "As sure as I'll die some day. Good night, Katie."

*   *   *

Black Roger, Petey Daley's hired muscle, answered the door to The Dead Rabbits' Headquarters. He smiled, "'ullo, Ted."

"Roger, how be ye?" Ted asked.

Roger shrugged. "Me knuckles hurt a bit. Nothing more."

"Heard ye lost Maxie."

Black Roger nodded sadly, "Aye. Blind Billy, Tommy Yank, and Eugene, too."

Ted shook his head. "Shame. How's Petey taking it?"

Roger shrugged. "Nothing a little whiskey can't repair. Just don't mention them to him."

"I understand."

"Come on in, then," Roger said. Ted followed Black Roger into The Dead Rabbits' Headquarters. Cartons of stolen merchandise were stacked eight-high against each cracked and peeling wall: cartons of clothing, furs, silverware, food and liquor. Dozens of gang members slept on scattered mats. The building reeked of cigar smoke, urine, and alcohol.

Upon an archway which Black Roger led Ted through, someone had scrawled "The Grand Bluudy Ballroom". Entering a larger, more cavernous, room, Ted saw Petey Daley straddling the cannon. A crate of premium whiskey sat by his side.

"Aye! Enter, friend! Here!" Petey tossed an unopened bottle of whiskey to Ted.

Ted caught the bottle. "Thank ye." He uncorked the bottle with his teeth and sipped. "Ah, the best, Petey."

"Always," Petey said with a wink. "What can I do fer ye, Teddy?"

After another sip, Ted approached the most feared man in The Five Points. "Petey, ye know I'm not the type of man to hold a person to an obligation made under duress. So I'm requesting…"

Petey slid off the cannon. He stepped over to Ted and poked his chest with his forefinger. "Ye saved my bloody life, today. And ye have always been good to me and my boys. Name it and I'll do whatever it is, in memory of Max, Gene, Blind Billy, and Tom Yank."

"God bless 'em," Ted said softly.

As Ted gave Petey his request, Black Roger anticipated Petey's command. He stepped into a rear storeroom and grabbed an unopened crate of whiskey. He brought it into "The Grand Bluudy Ballroom".

Wee Petey frowned. "Is that all ye want from me?"

"That's it," Ted replied.

Petey shook his head. "Nay. Then I won't do it." Petey continued shaking is head, until he added, "Not unless ye take a case of me whiskey."

Ted grinned and extended his hand. "Done."

"Aye, done!" The two men shook hands.

Black Roger handed the crate to Ted. But then Ted turned once again. "Petey, one other thing."

"Go on."

"Have ye got a new set of hair clippers and a shaving razor? I'm looking an awful fright these days."

*   *   *

It was only a few days before Christmas, but on Friday morning the air was infused by unseasonable, balmy breezes and brilliant sunshine. Seagulls cawed and circled in the warmth of New York Harbor. Along the East Side docks, stacked crates of fish stank. The barrels of viscera and shucked oysters stank. The garbage stank. The river stank.

Harbormaster Amos Piel was fending off dozens of sailors and dockworkers at Peck Slip. Rumor was running rampant that the whaling ship, Augustus, had sunk forty miles east of Montauk, and that all aboard had perished.

"I've not heard any such news!" the grey, mutton chopped Harbormaster announced. "To the best of my knowledge, there have been no sinkings in the area. And I would be one of the first to know."

But the sailors protested.

"Nay!" one of them shouted. "I was on the clipper, Andromeda, and we all seen the terrible wreckage."

The men gasped. Until then, nobody had claimed to witness the sinking.

The man continued, "Was horrible! Corpses floating about, islands of blubber as far as the eye can see. I shiver just to think of it."

The Harbormaster put his fists on his hips. "What clipper Andromeda? I've no record of a clipper..."

"Twas the worst shipwreck I've ever seen," the man went on. "The wreckage was spread for miles. We thought we heard someone cry out, but when we sailed into the middle of it all, we realized she must've gone down forever." He wiped a tear from his eye. "A few miles further, we found a piece of her hull. And on it was the name Augustus."

"Oh no! Heavenly Father!" a sailor exclaimed. "My brother-in-law was aboard that whaler! Oh, Lord! Lord!" Several sailors went to console him.

The Harbormaster raised his arms. "Cease this, right now! There is no official word from anyone about a sinking! I cannot emphasize..."

A young man in an oversized bowler joined the crowd, and announced, "The reporters are here! The Sun, Leslie's Illustrated! They heard about the sinking of the Augustus."

Amos Piel put down his hands, shock on his face. "Newspapermen! My God!"

The young man went on. "The reporters say they got word of witnesses, and that the Navy is out there fetching the bodies. Reports are going over the telegraph lines! The blubber and whale oil had somehow ignited. No survivors! No survivors!"

Amos Piel shook his head. "Dreadful, dreadful!" He stifled an urge to cry. He looked at the mournful crowd. "Aye, men, for those of you who wish to pray or notify kin, you are free to go. I know I shall be praying."

Some sailors walked slowly to a local chapel. Others raced through the streets to spread the tragic news: The Augustus had sunk and all aboard were drowned.

*   *   *

The sockets of Cyril Stephens' eyes struggled desperately to prevent their eyeballs from popping out. His thin lips, however, made no attempt to keep the froth from spilling onto his chin. "Where is the little wench?" he boomed. "Where's Katie?" His jowls quivered.

Actually, Katie was already in the building and hanging up her coat. However, Cyril could not see the little woman through the crowd. "You, bouncer," Cyril yelled to one of his men, "go to Orange Street and fetch Katie!"

"I'm here," Katie said miserably, from the entrance.

Cyril spun around, his nostrils flaring. "Where have you been? Do you know the time?" He stormed over to tiny Katie. "Are you deaf? Do you know the time?" He backhanded Katie across the face. "Answer me!"

Katie hardly moved, except for the involuntary release of a tear. She said softly, "Aye, Cyril. Tis time for me to die." She walked past the pimp and headed for the stairway.

Cyril raised a forefinger like an aimed pistol. "Listen to me, Katie Cunnigham, if dying is what you're after, dying is what you'll get, if you're late again tomorrow."

Cyril swiped a bottle of whiskey from the bar and joined Superintendent Connery at a table. "Trouble, Cyril?" Connery asked with feigned interest, as he helped himself to a drink.

"Yes, trouble," Cyril replied, downing a shot of whiskey. "The little strumpet will be my death. Mark my words." He poured himself another.

*   *   *

A young man of clean-shaven good looks wiped his thick spectacles at the bar of The Suicide Hall. He seemed intimidated by the hurly-burly atmosphere.

"What'll ye have?" the bartender asked, rather impatiently.

"Oh!" the young man exclaimed, in a startled way. He wiped the sweat from his completely bald head. "Just a pint, please. Beer." He rummaged miserly through his change purse and placed a few coins on the bar.

The obese bartender slopped the beverage down before the customer.

After taking a sip of the warm, bitter beer, the customer requested, "Tell me something, sir, if you would."

"Aye?"

"In Philadelphia, where I'm from, I saw a business card for this establishment. And I made some inquiries." The young man looked around nervously before he whispered, "Well, I heard that women actually commit self-slaughter on these premises."

"Aye?" the bartender asked.

"Is it true?"

The bartender nodded, "And aye!"

Looking as if he'd just swallowed a bitter pill, the customer grimaced. "Awful. Awful." With an awestruck expression, the young man asked, "How...I'm sorry, but how can your work for such a place, when you know what goes on here?"

The bartender rested a pudgy hand on the bar. "It's a job. Understand? A job. Why? Have ye got a better job for me?"

"Oh, no, no," the young man stammered. "No, I'm sorry. I meant no offense."

"Now, you tell me something, then," the bartender said.

"Yes, sir."

"What do ye do for a living?"

Modestly, the customer replied, "I'm a doctor."

"Well, doctor," the bartender said, pushing the pint of beer closer to the customer, "I would advise ye to be quiet and drink yer medicine"

*   *   *

Petey Daley and Black Roger swaggered in The Suicide Hall. "Look for Connery," Petey instructed. The two separated and wove their way through the smoke-filled hall. Men sat in groups of two or four: some played faro, some watched the faro players, others gazed and judged the prostitutes leaning over the upper balconies.

Black Roger let out a sharp whistle and got Petey's attention. He tilted his head to the right, where Police Superintendent Connery and Cyril Stephens were sitting. Petey nodded.

"It's no easy job running this place, I can tell you," Cyril sighed.

Superintendent Connery growled, "Try being a Police Superintendent who has to listen to yer drivel! How much money do ye make? Spare me yer whinin!" He poured himself another drink.

Petey Daley sprang up beside Connery and cleared his throat. Connery did not have to look up at the standing Wee Petey. "Mr. Daley. How be ye? Have a drink!"

Petey pondered for a second, but then said, "Nay, Superintendent. But I need to talk with ye. Tis important."

Images of meat-cleaver swinging gangs flashed into Superintendent Connery's mind. "What is it, Petey? Troubles?"

Petey shrugged. "Not yet. That's why I need to speak with ye. Outside." Black Roger joined Petey at the table and smiled at the Superintendent. The rotted teeth encouraged Connery to excuse himself and follow the pair out into the street.

*   *   *

"Smile, Katie. Come on, now!" Cynthia Stuart urged, digging her elbow into Katie's side. Cynthia and Katie were in the center of the largest balcony of girls; girls who blew kisses, exposed their breasts, and lifted their skirts: invitations to a brief repast of flesh.

"What's wrong with you?" Cynthia asked. "Are you ill?"

Katie refused to separate her chin from her collarbone. "Aye. I'm sick of this life."

Cynthia caught the eye of a patron by the bandstand. She pinched her nipples and blew a kiss. The customer nodded with approval but then turned his attention to a card game at a nearby table. "What's that you said?" she asked.

Katie's pout swelled. "A man was coming to take me away. Now, he's drowned."

Cynthia curled a lip. "A sailor?"

"Aye."

"Good for the bastard!" Cynthia exclaimed. "Sailors will promise you the world—THE WORLD—but they don't come back."

Katie's pout trembled. "Nay, Frank was different. He was coming back for me."

"Certainly," Cynthia said without sincerity.

"Tis true!" Katie declared. "O, I wish I were dead!" Katie hid her eyes behind a sleeve and raced away. "I wish to die!"

*   *   *

Although Ted had been to The Suicide Hall often, he never knew what to expect each time he entered. Taking a deep breath, he opened the door. He angled to the left, massaging the back of his neck as he walked. There was a pained expression on his face, as he ordered, "Brandy, sir."

The young, bespectacled doctor noted Ted's pain. After sipping his beer, he cautiously asked, "What ails you, sir?"

Ted snapped, "What business is it of yers?"

The bartender gave Ted his drink and took his money. He told him, "Our bald young friend, here, is a bloody doctor."

Ted sipped his brandy. He looked at the doctor who seemed sorry he'd asked Ted anything. "Forgive me, sir," Ted said. " 'twas a damp night, last night. And I was out and about in it."

The doctor nodded. "So you have a cramp in your neck?"

Ted nodded painfully. "Aye."

With a little confidence, the doctor said, "Would you allow me to take a quick look? Don't worry, I won't bill you."

Ted shrugged, but that seemed to cause him pain. "Aye, go on."

After pinching and probing the back of Ted's neck, and dishing out a handful of "Mm-hmms", the doctor announced, "That's a neck bone that's out of place, you have there."

"Bugger," Ted sighed. "Will I need to go to the hospital?"

The doctor shook his head. "Turn around." Ted did as instructed. The doctor placed one hand on the back of Ted's neck, with the other he reached around and firmly gripped Ted's fore-head. "This may hurt a bit." Sharply, the doctor pulled back Ted's head.

"JAY-zus!" Ted cried. After a second, the stunned look on his face was replaced by a small smile. He rotated his head. "Aye. That done it! That done it!" He shook the doctor's hand. "Yer a bloody genius. Bartender, give this man a proper drink!" He rotated his head again. "Tis like bloody new!"

The bartender chimed in, "It's too bad the doctor can't do any-thing fer the poor bastards that drowned this morning."

"Who drowned"? Ted asked.

"The whaling ship Augustus. It went down this morning. All members were lost," the bartender answered.

Ted frantically looked around. "O, my God," he exclaimed. He asked the bartender, "Where's Katie Cunningham? I must speak to her! O, Lord!"

*   *   *

Cynthia Stuart did not follow Katie. She continued posing for the men, hoping she could make some money. Then she saw Katie sitting at the near end of the bar. "What are you doing down there, Katie?" she shouted. Katie didn't reply. She then saw Katie pull a phial from her bodice. Katie removed the cap and swal-lowed the contents. "Oh, Lord, no!" Cynthia screamed. *"Katie!"*

*   *   *

Outside the temperature was still deceiving the populace that spring was near. Ice and snow were melting, forming rivulets along every curbside and in every crack on the walkways. "Ye have my attention," Superintendent Connery told Petey Daley. "Tell me, what's afoot?"

"I suggest ye go down to the East Side docks, Superintendent," Petey said. "A ship has gone down near Montauk. Most of the dockworkers are either in chapel or running about, looking for information. I hear The Daybreak Boys are going' to take advantage of this and plunder the warehouses."

Connery stopped twirling the end of his mustache. "The Daybreak Boys, eh? O, yes, I seem to remember those lads!" His eyes narrowed into little slits. "Let me ask ye, Petey, hypothetically, of course: Let's say ye were the leader of a vicious, thieving gang. Ye hear about possible unguarded warehouses, some of which might contain some valuables. Tell me, why would ye tell the police that another gang was going to raid them warehouses, instead of robbing them yerself?"

Petey rubbed his chin and smiled. "Well, hy-po-thet-i-cal-ly, of course, I would assume that nothing in them warehouses pleases my fancy, Superintendent."

"I see." The Superintendent knew he was being taken on a wild goose chase. The Daybreak Boys, after a rash of bungling, followed by stepped-up river security during the fifties and sixties, were all but extinct. And, even if they had still been around as the premier dock and warehouse raiders, The Daybreak Boys only committed their crimes at one time of day: daybreak. It was obvious that Petey Daley wanted the Superintendent out of the neighborhood. "Thank ye, Petey," Connery said, tipping his hat. "I'll go catch the miscreants." he jumped onto his pony and trap, and headed north. Petey grabbed Black Roger's elbow, "Come, Rog, let's go find our friend, Ted."

*   *   *

Like piglets squirming for position near their mother's nipples, men clustered at the near end of the bar. The commotion caught

Cyril's attention. This, coupled with Superintendent Connery's abrupt departure, rattled the pimp's nerves. "Bloody Hell," he muttered. He rose from his seat and waddled his corpulence toward the excitement.

A tear-streaked Cynthia Stuart craned her neck over the crowd as she tried to make her way toward the bar. "Katie!" she cried. She jostled the men, "Let me through!" But the moving sea of men blocked her path with mindless efficiency. That is, until Cyril barreled past, clearing a way for her to follow.

When they got to the epicenter of the action, they saw the young doctor pressing his fingers on Katie Cunningham's jugular vein. Katie Cunningham, little girl Katie, former employee at Cyril Stephen's The Suicide Hall, lay flat on her back in the sawdust, an empty phial in her hand. The doctor, open-mouthed with terror, took his hand off her. He removed his jacket and draped it over Katie's face. "This girl is dead," he announced.

"No!" Cynthia shrieked. "O, no!"

Cyril's breathing grew heavy. He asked, "Poison?"

The young doctor picked up the phial and sniffed it. "Strychnine. Lord."

Ted stared down at Katie. "Bastard."

Cyril wiped a tear from his eye. He placed his hand on his heart, "Gentlemen, many of the girls who come to my establishment have been on the decline for so long that..."

Ted erupted, "She was only thirteen when she came here, you parasite! Bastard!" Ted pounded Cyril with an uppercut to the nose, breaking it.

The bouncers prepared to rush Ted, but Petey Daley and smiling Black Roger stood in front of them and, without saying a word, convinced them not to interfere. Well aware of who Petey and Roger were, the bouncers distracted themselves with the change in their pockets.

Cyril, like a customer who imbibed too much, stumbled back several paces before landing on his back unconscious. Clouds of sawdust rose in the aftermath. Many patrons gathered around the fallen pimp; others shied away from the violence, even as far as fleeing the establishment.

The doctor stood up and restrained Ted from inflicting further damage. "No, sir, please! Calm down." The bartender reached over the bar and grabbed Ted by the shoulders, pinning him to the bar. "Just stay there, friend," the doctor said. Ted didn't put up much resistance as the doctor walked over to the unconscious Cyril. Bending on one knee, he probed the bloodied nose.

"Can you mend it?" a customer asked.

The doctor shook his head. "No, he will need surgery. Someone help me load him onto my pony and cart. I'll take him to the hospital." He turned to Ted. "Have you collected your senses enough to pick up that poor young girl and put her on my cart, as well?"

Ted bit his lower lip, then he nodded, "Aye."

One of the patrons volunteered to help the doctor move Cyril outside.

After the bartender released his hold, Ted walked over and crossed himself sadly over Katie's body. He then bent down, and, making sure the doctor's jacket remained over Katie's face, lifted the weight over his shoulder.

The moment he got outside, Ted was blinded by the sunlight. When his eyes adjusted to it, he stepped over to the cart. He gently placed the body next to Cyril. "Doctor," he said.

The doctor, who was already in the riding seat, said, "Yes, sir?"

Ted plaintively asked, "Please, sir, may I ride with ye to the ferry to Potter's Field? The girl has no family, and I was one of the few friends she had." Ted mournfully added, "I'd hate to see the child buried alone."

Wee Petey and Black Roger emerged from the brothel. The grins on their faces no longer seemed menacing. They seemed very pleased with themselves. Petey tipped his bowler to the doctor.

The doctor looked at Petey. "Certainly, sir." He then said to Ted. "Climb on."

Petey called out, "Be sure ye show the good doctor which way to go, Teddy!"

Ted waved in acknowledgment, and sat beside the doctor.

The doctor put the whip to the pony. They proceeded at a brisk pace along the muddy street.   An elderly woman paused on the corner of Mulberry and Spring Streets, and observed the shabby death cart as it approached her. She crossed herself as she strained to see the bodies. Her effort, however, was in vain: all she could see were the splayed feet of a man and a girl.

Looking up, she observed the two respectable-looking men on the riding seat. They seemed to be having a grand old time, laughing at the top of their lungs. She frowned, "Some people have no respect for the dead."

            *   *   *

The terror, like fire in a pile of dry leaves, spread swiftly and completely consumed whatever it touched along the piers on the Lower East Side. Grown men—sailors, dockworkers, and naval officers—ran screaming along the planks. "Tis a specter," some cried.

"The work of the devil!" others shouted.

"Ghost!"

"A blessing!"

"Demon!"

"A miracle!"

Harbormaster Amos Piel stood dumbly on Peck Slip. Panicked men raced by him in waves. "Holy Jesus," he mumbled.

Above the cries of men and cawing of gulls, Amos Piel could hear the creaking of the great bow. He heard the sails fluttering in the warm breezes, along with the snapping of cables and squeaking of pulleys and tackles.

The grey wind-worn sails dropped gracefully, unveiling the brilliant sun behind them. Amos shaded his eyes with his hand. He watched the men climb down he ratlins and shimmy along the yards. Some of the sailors looked weary as they munched on their hardtack or slurped their burgoo, but most of them looked happy to reach port. No matter what their expressions were, they looked real. They were not ghosts or demons or angels. They were men whose blood coursed beneath their suntanned and salt-encrusted skins.

"Ha-HA!" the harbormaster cried. He tossed his cap into the air. "She didn't go down! She didn't go down! Ha-HA!"

Indeed, as the ship's enormous black anchor splashed into the East River, the Augustus had made it home. Safe.

*   *   *

At Canal Street, Superintendent Connery turned his carriage west. He realized it was fruitless to head to the docks—nothing was going to happen there, at least, not by The Daybreak Boys. However, he thought it best to return to the precinct for two reasons: first, to be there as soon as the crime—or whatever it was Petey Daley was up to—would be reported, and second, and more importantly, to have an alibi as to his whereabouts during that time, and avoid implication.

"I don't want to know what's going to happen," he grumbled. He put the whip to the pony's rump. "What I don't know can't hurt me. Yet."

As he directed his pony and trap toward the precinct, he saw a striking, red-haired young woman standing by its entrance. She was tall and slender, with pale skin and freckles. Her deep green eyes crinkled with her broad smile. "No woman ever looked happier to see me," Connery thought, as he returned the smile and waved to his fiancée, Elizabeth Shaw.

The Superintendent jumped onto the cobblestones. "What are ye doing here?" he asked, as he took Elizabeth's hand and kissed it.

"Why? Aren't ye glad to see me?" Elizabeth playfully asked.

Connery chuckled. "Of course, I am." He put his arm around her waist. "Tis just a surprise, that's all."

"I'm glad I surprised ye, then," she said. "Actually, the florist is not far from here: on Allen Street. We want good flowers fer our wedding, don't we? And this gentleman is supposed to be the best. After that, I took the chance that ye would be here."

"I see," Michael said with a nod. "And, tell me, how much is this florist going to cost me?"

"Not much. What's the difference? Yer a big copper with lots of money!"

"That's right, I am," Michael quickly said. And that's how he was going to play it, he determined. Just as Petey Daley had sent him on a wild goose chase for his own good, Michael would serve his wife's and his own best interest by misdirecting Elizabeth with his answers about money. *"Where did this two hundred dollars come from, Mike?"* she'll someday ask. *"O, from the Policeman's Fund,"* he'll answer. Or *"From the Captains' and Roundsmen Benevolence League."* Or *"A reward from City Hall for my efforts during blah, blah, blah."* It didn't matter what he would tell her, as long as it wasn't the truth. "Yes, ma'm, that's right," he repeated.

✶   ✶   ✶

A few blocks from the pier, the pony and trap came to a halt in a deserted alley. Ted turned around and looked at the pair lying in the cart. He said, "Poor Katie."

"Aye, the poor young lass." The young man removed his jacket from Katie's face. "Must be warm under this."

Katie opened her eyes. "Pah!" she blurted, waving her hand before her face. "Were ye trying to suffocate me?" She smiled as she sat up. "We made it."

"Aye, we made it," Ted said.

Katie laughed. She crept up to the riding seat and massaged the bald head before her. "Look at ye, Rudy. Yer a sight!"

"Do ye like it?" Rudy asked. "Took Teddy, here, three-quarters of an hour to cut and shave me hair."

"T'will probably grow back in three-quarters of a month," Ted said. "The good doctor has a healthy head, except for the lack of a brain within."

Rudy rubbed his chin. "Tis the beard that will take long to grow but...Aye."

"How much has our friend for us?" Ted asked.

"Ah!" Katie exclaimed. She scampered toward Cyril. "He always keeps his money in this breast pocket." She rummaged through the brown plaid jacket until she found the purse. Bringing it to Rudy and Ted, she remarked, "Twas busy last night. Should be a great sum in there."

Ted ripped open the lavender purse. He began counting the bills.

"Push the bugger off," Rudy told Katie.

"Aye" Katie said. Bracing her back against the riding seat, Katie placed a foot on each of Cyril's shoulders. With a quick thrust, the pimp was pushed off the cart and into a pile of dung. "Good-bye, bastard."

"Jesus!" Ted exclaimed. He flashed a smile so wide it creased the scar by his eye. "There's over one hundred dollars in here. Hee-hee!" He quickly counted out 60 dollars and gave it to Katie, who promptly placed the money down the front of her dress.

"Come let's be quick!" Katie exclaimed, as her youthful anticipation could not be held in check any longer.

"Aye," Ted agreed. The cart quickly emerged from the shadows of the alleyway, and into the bright, pungent air of the thoroughfare.

As they clip-clopped toward the docks, Ted turned to Katie and asked, "How'd ye like the strychnine?"

Katie licked the inside of her mouth. "Twas tasty! What was in it?"

"Best ye ask the doctor," Ted answered. "After all, it was his concoction. He spent most of the night sampling it fer himself."

Rudy said, "One part rum, one part water, and one part honey. Sounds poisonous enough doesn't it?" He put the whip to the pony's rump. "Gee!"

Though usually a busy port, the warm weather brought even denser crowds to South Street, from Pike Street clear down to the Battery. Whalers, schooners, and clipper ships bobbed dumbly in the East River. Dockworkers busily loaded or unloaded the vessels. The fish and produce stands were doing tremendous business.

Two of the old-fashioned Hot Corn Girls, young and pretty, the few left of their trade, carried cedar-staved buckets filled with ears of the steaming hot vegetable through the crowd. They sang their traditional song:

Hot Corn! Hot Corn!
Here's your lily white corn!
All you that's got money—
Poor me that's got none
Come buy my lily hot corn
And let me go home!

A group of businessmen sat on wooden crates and greedily devoured foot-long oysters by a seafood stand. Two little boys contemplated the complexity of a coconut.

Ted called out to a sailor. "Lad! Where can I find the Augustus?"

The tar laughed, "You must be jesting! Just follow that crowd over there!" He pointed toward an excited mob that clustered by a pier a quarter of a mile down. "Go and witness the miracle of the Augustus."

"Thank ye," Rudy said.

As they approached Peck Slip, Ted remarked, "Ye can always count on the Rabbits. Petey's boys did a good job spreadin' the rumor."

"I would dare say!" Rudy laughed heartily, noting how many people were gathering to view the "miracle".

A young man of average height stood at the perimeter of the crowd. Blonde-haired, slender, the youth looked this way then that. He carried a gunnysack over his shoulder. Ted picked him out immediately. "Katie, there's yer lad."

Katie smiled so hard she squeezed tears out of the corners of her eyes. She softly replied, "Yes." After taking in the sight of her lover, she suddenly furrowed her brow. "Here, Ted, how did you know that was Frank?"

Ted shrugged. "He's young. Handsome. He's not looking for a wife or a whore: he's looking for someone he loves."

Katie laughed. As the cart neared Frank, she stood up, "Frank! Frank! Over here!" She waved her hands over her head.

Frank turned and saw his young love. He put the sack down and eagerly approached the cart, which was slowing to a halt.

Katie embraced Ted and then Rudy. "I shall never forget you men. And what ye did for me. I don't know what would have hap..."

"Oh no," Ted exclaimed. "None of this sentimental nonsense. Just go to yer lad, and get to where ye want to be. I haven't the stomach fer this lovey-dovey malarkey."

Rudy chuckled. "Aye. This from the man who can tell when a lad is 'looking for someone he loves'." The last few words were more warbled than spoken.

Ted reached under the riding seat and pulled out Katie's carpet-bag. "Don't forget this."

Aye!" She took the bag, kissed both men on the cheek, and jumped off the cart. The space which separated the young couple actually seemed to pull them together. Katie leapt into Frank's arms.

Ted nudged Rudy. "Let's be off."

"Aye." Rudy whipped the pony, and the cart made its way up South Street. "Don't forget to return the clippers and razor to Petey," Rudy told Ted.

Once Frank put Katie down, he asked, "How have you been? I've been thinking about you for all these weeks, Katie."

For one of the few times in her life, Katie Cunningham blushed. "I'm well. If it weren't fer these two gentle.." Katie turned, only to see that Rudy and Ted had disappeared. "Now where did they…" A look of suspicion crossed Katie's face. Then it quickly vanished when she realized she'd been had. In seconds, she was beside her-self laughing.

"What's so funny?" Frank asked with a smile.

Katie shook her head. Through her laughter, she asked, "Would ye give me my bag?" Frank bent down to get the bag and handed it to Katie. "The bastards," she said. Katie looked in the bag and saw that the compartment she had sewn closed was now open. Of the money she had in there, only ten dollars remained. "The thieving bastards," she laughed. However, she found a note inside that read:

DID YOU THINK WE WOULDN'T CHARGE A FEE?
LOVE,
R&T

"Something wrong, Katie?" Frank asked.

Katie, little girl Katie, free to go with the man she loved, Katie, shook her head with a smile that exposed just about every tooth in her mouth. "Those bastards! Those rotten, wonderful bastards," she announced.

END OF THE SECOND BOOK